Stacey Roberts
the Green Girl

Stacey Roberts the Green Girl

SL Armstrong

To order additional copies of this book, contact:
Xlibris
800-056-3182
www.Xlibrispublishing.co.uk
Orders@Xlibrispublishing.co.uk
776432

CONTENTS

CHAPTER ONE

Medical Volunteer

It was a cold Octobers night as Stacey was walking home from college, as always, she was on her own. Stacey was a shy reserved sort of girl, she had short blonde hair that she kept in a ponytail. She wore a pair of thick round glasses that she always had on, she was wearing a pair of blue colored jeans and a Star Wars tee shirt, at both college and school, she was always looked on as a geek with very few friends. At first, Stacey didn't really like it as the other girls at school began to consider her a freak, but since she had finished school and gone to college things had been different. She was still a bit of a loner, but the other students had just left her alone and not picked on her.

As she was walking past the small newsagents at the top of her street her mobile phone started to ring, quickly she rushed to get it out of her bag and answered it, "hello who's this?" She said in a soft and low voice.

"Hi Stacey," a female voice answered.

"Hi mum," she replied back in a warm voice.

"How was college sweetheart?" Her mum asked in a kind voice.

Stacey smiled, "It was good, thanks mum. he tutor thinks that I should go to university and do a computer science course."

Her mum smiled over the phone, "That's wonderful, Stacey! Well done. Would you mind doing me a favor please?" Stacey knew what her mum was going to ask this always happened every time she finished college. "Would you mind going to the shop on your way passed home and get me some milk, please? Your brother forgot."

Stacey pulled a face, "Yes ok mum don't worry I'll get some milk."

Her mum then smiled again. "Good girl, Stacey. I knew that you wouldn't let me down."

She then hung up and the phone went dead, Stacy then put in back inside her ruck stack and made her way to the shop. Once she got inside she made her way towards the milk, as she did this she noticed a sign on the front of the shop's door, looking at it read, "Need medical volunteers to test a new serum, apply now and transform into a new person."

Interested she took her phone out of her bag and using the camera began taking a few shots of the poster, once she did this she paid for the milk and began the short walk home. When she got in she could see that her mum was waiting for her.

"Nice to see you again Stacey," she said as she took the milk out of her hand and placed it in the fridge. "Thank you for getting the milk you're a star and I don't know what I would do without you?"

Stacey smiled as she looked at her, her mother looked like her, she was five feet six inches tall, but unlike her daughter, she had short light brown hair and didn't wear glasses.

Stacey smiled at her and opened her bag, "This is the University application form that I've got to fill out mum, I was also thinking as well, I've seen an advertisement on the shop's door tonight for a medical volunteer, what do you think?"

Her mum's face dropped in bewilderment. "I thought that you wanted to go to University Stacey?" she said in a puzzled voice.

Stacey gave her a slight smile, "I do mum, but that won't be until next year. I'll need a part-time job until then and this could be perfect please let me try it?"

The older woman looked at her daughter and smiled, "If that's what you want to do before university then why don't you give it a go? But be very careful Stacy. I have heard bad things about those places."

Stacey smiled as she ran upstairs, "What could go wrong mum, I doubt that they would use anything dangerous on me?"

CHAPTER TWO

Medical Center

A few months had passed since Stacey had been thinking about becoming a medical volunteer. Once it was January she had applied online, once her application had been cleared she along with a few other applicants were picked up from their homes and transported to the medical center. Stacey, when she arrived, couldn't believe her eyes, the center was a huge glass building in the middle of nowhere, covering the building was a thick blanket of both barbed and razor wire, looking at it made Stacey think that she and the others were in prison, she now was having second thoughts. As she and the other volunteers were lining up outside to be checked she noticed a young female scientist coming out of the building, she was in her early thirties and had pale white skin, she had dark brown eyes and medium red colored hair. She slowly made her way towards the crowd, when she had done this she began to speak.

"Welcome to you all and thank you for volunteering your time with us, my name is Doctor Sarah Young and I'm in charge of this center, as you are all aware by now you have been asked to test out a new product that has become available this new product is a super serum."

Stacey grew a bit nervous as she heard this, what have I done? She started thinking to herself as she saw the other application moving towards the door of the center, she stood by watching them go in, as she did this she could feel something or someone rubbing against her arm, she then turned and looked straight into the eyes of a young man, he was medium built, with pale blue eyes and short dirty blonde hair and was wearing a pair of blue colored glasses.

"Hi," the young man said to her in a warm friendly voice, "Are you nervous? There is no need to be," he said smiling, Stacey smiled back and nodded her head, the young man then looked at her again. "Please allow me to introduce myself, my name is Ben Fox and you are?"

Stacey looked at Ben and smiled, "My name is Stacey Roberts."

Ben smiled at her again this time showing her a set of gleaming white teeth. "Stacey, lovely name for such a pretty girl. Look, there is no need to be nervous about this place."

Stacey looked at him and gave him a puzzled look. "How do you know?"

Ben gave her a smile. "I know of people who have been here before and let's just say that when they come out they are changed."

Stacey smiled at him. "You seem like a nice guy, Ben. Have you got a girlfriend?"

Ben gave her a quick shake of his head. "No, I haven't," he paused for a moment. "To be honest with you that's why I'm here."

Stacey gave him a smile. "Let's hope that changes for both of us."

Ben smiled back and the two of them followed each other inside the center, over the next few months Ben and Stacey became close, they started helping each other with problems, one-night Ben asked Stacey if the two of them could start dating, at first Stacey was a bit afraid of that like with most things Ben talked her into it. The next day Doctor Young called them both into her office.

"Mr. Fox, Miss Roberts," she said in a polite friendly voice. "We would like to begin testing you with the serum today, how do you feel about that?"

Ben looked at Stacey and she looked at him. "Doctor," Stacy then said. "We both accept this offer."

Doctor young smiled at them both. "Good then let us begin."

CHAPTER THREE

Stacey's Transformation

It was getting late in the afternoon as both Ben and Stacey were getting ready to go into the lab, they were both wearing a blue and white gown and they also had their glasses off. Ben turned to Stacey and smiled at her. "Whatever happens in there, know that you will always be the same person in my eyes babe," he said as he held her hand.

Stacey leaned over and kiss Ben gently on his lips. As they both were doing this they both heard a voice.

"Stacey, Doctor Young is ready for you now."

"Ok, I'm coming now," she called back outside to the assistant.

Ben smiled. "Best not to keep the doctor waiting babe."

Stacey threw her arms around him and then rushed off outside where the assistant was waiting, he then took her through to the lab where waiting for her was Doctor Young.

In her hand was a vial of green colored liquid, Stacey looked at it in wonder, Doctor young then looked at her and smiled. "Welcome Stacy are you ready for this procedure?"

Stacey smiled at her, "Yes, I am doctor," she said in a warm voice.

"Good," Doctor young then said. "Would you mind taking a seat for me?" she said this as she pointed to a chair.

Stacy sat down on it, as she was sitting down she noticed that she was fastened down to it. Doctor Young came over to her, she was now wearing a surgeon's mask and goggles, in her hand was a syringe full of the green liquid that Stacy had seen in the vial before. Gently Doctor Young injected the needle into Stacey's arm, she did this until every last drop of liquid was used. For a moment after nothing really happened, then all of a sudden Stacey felt strange and she closed her eyes. Doctor Young pulled back as she noticed that Stacey was growing in height, her blonde hair became longer, and her skin color changed from pale white to a light green. Stacey's eyes flicked open as she saw Doctor Young standing afar.

"Doctor," she said in a strange voice. "What happened and was the procedure a success?"

Doctor Young came forward, "I don't know how to say this to you Stacey, but you are completely changed."

Stacey then began to laugh. "Changed what do you mean changed?"

"Take a look for yourself Miss," one of the assistant's said as he handed her a mirror.

Stacey took a good look at herself and then dropped it in shock. "What the hell has happened to me and what have you done?" she said in alarm.

Doctor Young then came up to her and put her one of her hands over her arm. "Don't worry. Stacey," she said in a soothing warm voice. "This is just a side effect I'm sure that it will wear off after a few days."

Stacey pulled away in disgust. "I'm just a weapon to you?"

The doctor then started laughing. "Yes, you are now, these tests that we carried out we want to test them on soldiers, but the military wouldn't allow us to do that, so we had to use civilians like yourself to use as lab rats. The serum that has been used on yourself has proven to be a success and now you, like Ben, and the rest of the volunteers will be used by the military in their super soldier program." Stacey didn't like the sound of that and began to look for an escape. "You really shouldn't think about escaping now my dear, you now belong to us."

CHAPTER FOUR

Escape!

Stacey was looking around the lab for an escape, she couldn't believe what Doctor Young had told her, that the experiments had just been to use people as super soldiers for the military.

"Come on my dear," the doctor then said as she held out her hand. "Don't be foolish, there is no escape."

As she was saying this there was a flash of bright orange light followed by a loud bang. Stacey spied her change using her new-found strength she threw Doctor Young over her shoulder and onto the floor, she also hit one of the assistants standing next to her and she got another assistant by her neck.

"Please," the assistant begged. "Please don't hurt me I'll do anything you want."

Stacey brought the assistant close so that she could look her in the eyes. "Help me escape from this place then and I'll let you go."

"Escape," the assistant said softly. "No one has ever escaped from here."

Stacey then began to hold her neck tight. "Please, get me out of here or you are going to die."

The assistant started panicking. "Ok, please let me go and I'll show you how you can get out of here."

Stacey then let her go, the assistant then made her way to Doctor Young's body, who had been knocked out cold. She then started going through her pockets until she found what she was looking for.

"Here," the assistant said as she handed over a security card to Stacey. "This is Doctor Young's pass card, it allows staff access to come in and out of the building when they wish, here take it."

Stacey grabbed the card from the woman and hid it inside her gown which now had become ripped. She then looked at the woman and nodded her head as she made her way towards the lab's door, as she was about to leave she heard the assistant calling out.

"You aren't thinking of leaving dressed as you, are you?" she asked.

Stacey turned and walked slowly towards her, as she was doing this one of her green hands was now in a fist. "What are you suggesting?" she asked in a hard voice, the assistant backed away from her.

"Why don't you take Doctor Young uniform?" Stacey then smiled at the women.

"Thank you, that sounds like a good idea," as she said this she hit her knocking the assistant out.

Stacey then made her way towards Doctor Young's body and began undressing her, once she was finished doing this she began to get dressed. She had the goggles on, her lab coat, a pair of latex gloves and her hair net and the surgeons mask, she then left the lab leaving both the assistant's and Doctor Young, as she passed through the door she started to think to herself about Ben.

"I can come back for him later, first things first, I've got to get myself out of here."

As she exited the lab she noticed that the corridor that she and her walked thought was clear on the other side was the exit. She began to run and as she was doing this she noticed that she now had increased speed. It took her fifteen minutes to reach the exit. She reached into her pocket and pulled out the security card inserting it into the lock, the door opened, and she was free. She stepped outside, and the air hit her, she then began to run straight for a wooded area just outside the medical center. As she ran, she threw the lab coat off her shoulders leaving it lying in a puddle of water. Not watching what she was doing or where she was going, Stacey tripped up and ended up flying. When she came to from her fall, she noticed that one of her legs was bleeding, she also noticed that she was by a steam. Looking at her leg she noticed that the blood was colored dark green not red, she also noticed that for some strange and unknown reason the large cut was healing. Not only had she developed super strength, she had also developed an increase in speed and a super healing factor. Once her leg was completely healed she made her way towards the stream, as she looked at her reflection in the water she noticed something, she wasn't a monster, no, she was now completely attractive, she had light colored green skin, dark green colored lips and eyes and long blonde hair. She then stood up as she admired herself.

"From this day forward," she said out loud, "I'm no longer Stacey Roberts, I'm The Green Girl."

CHAPTER FIVE

The Beach

It was a warm summer's afternoon at a public beach in Florida, as two young men were kicking a small blue colored football around by the sea, as they were kicking it closer to the sea one of them stopped and looked.

"Hey Ben, why did you stop?" his friend asked.

Ben turned and faced him and instructed his friend. "Look over there John and tell me what you see."

Both young men were in their early twenties, Ben was tall and slim and had short blonde hair whilst his friend John was around the same height but had short jet-black hair, they were both wearing a pair of blue and black swimming trunks.

John stood next to Ben and began to look towards the sea. "What I am looking for Ben?"

Ben began to point with a finger towards where the beach met the sea. "John," he shouted. "Are you blind, or is that the reason why you wear glasses?" John didn't like that comment, he didn't really like it when his friend made fun of him about his glasses or anything else.

He carried on looking, then he spotted what Ben was telling him about, lying on the beach on a sunbed near the sea, was a young woman. She had long light colored blonde hair and was wearing a light blue swimsuit, on her face she was wore a pair of black sunglasses, everything about the woman seemed normal apart from her light green colored skin.

John looked at Ben and gave him a smile. "God Ben, look at her, she is smoking hot." Ben gave his friend a smile back. "I told you, didn't I? We should come here more often, as there are always hot babes on this beach."

John gave Ben a playful punch to one of his arms. "Yeah Ben, but never this hot, I wonder who she is and if that's skin color is natural."

Ben looked at John and started laughing. "Don't know John," he said. "What I do know is that both you and me have just made a new friend." Saying that he raced towards her leaving John where he had been standing.

"Ben," John shouted at his friend. "Don't do anything stupid, we don't know what that woman is or where she has come from."

Ben either didn't listen or he was ignoring his friend, he just ran. As he made his way up to the sunbed he noticed that she was asleep and how attractive she was, it looked to him as if her green skin was glowing in the sun. Coming up to her, he looked down at her and the sunbed. She was well over six foot, besides her green skin, she had dark green colored lips and both her finger and toenails were also dark green in color. Ben was tempted to just give her a small peck on her cheek, but he didn't, he just stared at her. Without any warning just as Ben was about to say something the woman woke up. Ben nearly had a heart attack as the woman looked at him.

"Hey," she said in an English accent. "I didn't know that anyone else came here beside me."

She slowly got up from the sunbed and began to stretch both of her legs. Ben noticed that there wasn't a single hair on them both; all of her body was smooth. Seeing her get up from the sunbed John rushed down towards both her and Ben, when he got near them both he was out of breath. The woman looked at them both and both of her hands clenched into fists.

"So. there are two of you?" she said as she became angry. "Looks like my sunbathing will have to wait for a minute and what are you two doing, spying on me?!"

John looked at her and then lowered his head. "We didn't mean to spy on you, mam," he said as he was speaking for both himself and Ben. "We both, usually come to this beach often and it's full of women, but you are the first person that we have seen all day."

Ben nodded in agreement with this statement and smiled.

The women looked at them both. "So you aren't from the military then?"

Ben looked up at her. "No mam, we aren't/ We just live near the next block from this beach."

The woman then smiled and took the pair of sunglasses that she had been wearing off. She gave the young men a friendly smile and stared at them with a pair of dark green eyes. "Looks like you two are just a couple of young boys who are up for a good time. Am I right in asking you this?"

Ben and John looked at each other.

"We normally come here," John said nervously. "Because we both want to meet women."

The woman started laughing. "How very cute," she said in a joking voice. "Listen boys, why don't you hit the bars and clubs uptown and forget about seeing me here?"

The two boys then looked at each other and then ran off. After they had both gone the woman folded the sunbed that she was lying on and went back to her car. As she was walking up to the bank where her car was, she noticed the two young men sitting on the bank. Seeing them she walked slowly up to them both.

"Hey boys," she said smiling at them both as she came towards them. "I thought that you were both heading towards town?"

Ben looked at her. "We were miss," he said feeling stupid. "But then we remembered this beach is five miles from town."

The woman slowly walked away from the two and continued up the bank towards her car, she then stopped and turned around to face them both. "I could give you both a lift if you would like?"

The two young men looked at each other and smile. "Please miss that would be awesome of you."

The three of them walked up halfway to the bank, near there was a red Ford car, the woman unlocked the car doors and Ben and John got in. A few minutes later the woman got into the front seat and started the engine, the car zoomed away, and they were off. They hadn't been on the road for very long when the car stopped the woman turned around to face them both smiling.

"So, what are your names?" she asked them smiling.

"My names Ben," Ben said as he grinned. "And this is my friend the king of the geeks John, what is your name mam?"

The woman looked Ben in his eyes. "Call me Green Girl." she said as she turned around and started the engine.

CHAPTER SIX

Reliving the Past.

It was getting late in the afternoon as the red Ford zoomed into town. Inside the car both Ben and his friend John had decided to keep quiet, as they didn't want their new friend Green Girl, to get angry with them over stupid questions. Without warning the car stopped on a lay-by for no reason. The Green Girl turned her head towards the back seat of the car and looked at both Ben and John.

"Look, boys," she said in a pleasant voice. "I'm going to a friend's house tonight, would it be ok if I dropped you there, as she doesn't live too far from the town?"

Ben smiled at her. "That's fine with both of us, Green Girl," he laughed to himself as he said her name.

John his friend said nothing, he just sat there looking into space. Green Girl looked at him and he reminded her of when she had been Stacey Roberts. "Is your friend John ok Ben?" she asked him as she turned back around to the steering wheel and started the car up again.

"Don't worry about John," Ben said as he grinned. "He's usually shy when it comes to meeting new people, especial women like yourself."

Green girl again turned her head around, so that she could face them both. "Really, is that right?" She asked the young man. "When I was your age I was very much like your friend."

John's mouth dropped open. "Somehow, I find that hard to imagine," he said. "So what were you like when you were our age?" he asked in a confident voice.

Green Girl was now back in the driver's seat and was driving. "Back when I was your age, Ben," she said her with a low voice. "Before I became the Green Girl, my name had been Stacey Roberts. I was like your friend John, quiet, shy, low self-esteem but that all changed."

Ben sat up interested in what she was telling them both.

"How did it all change for you and how did you develop your green skin?"

"I was part of an experiment," she continued. "Me and so many other civilians, all so that the British military could use us as super soldiers in their next war." She stopped for a brief moment to give herself time to think about what she had just said. "I lost my family that day, my old life, the person that I used to be and my boyfriend Ben Fox." Ben and John sat up saying nothing as they listened carefully to what she told them.

She then paused.

"How terrible," Ben said. "What made you come to Florida?" he asked.

Green Girl then regained herself. "I just wanted to start a new life, I just wanted to leave my old one back home. England, free from the military and not to be used as an experiment, plus Florida is safe."

As she was saying this both Ben and John noticed that she was driving into a small residential town. There were quite a large number of small and large houses each with their own gardens. After they had been driving for a few minutes the car stopped outside a large house's drive. The Green Girl got out of the driver's seat and went and unlocked the back door to let both Ben and John out.

"Here we are boys," she said as they both got out of the car.

Ben look and smiled. "This looks like a private estate, God would you look at the size of that house?" Green Girl smiled at both him and Ben.

"Is this too far from the town for you both?"

Ben looked at her and smiled back. "This will be perfect for both of us. thank you for the lift."

Green Girl smiled. "You're both very welcome boys." They then waved goodbye to her and went on their way. Green Girl went up to the front door of the house and knocked. "Jennifer, are you in?"

As she waited the door slowly open and was answered by a young black woman. She had medium black hair, light black skin and was wearing a purple bra and pants.

"Green Girl," she said in an excited voice. "Your just in time for the next photo shoot bet you can't wait?"

Green Girl smile as she went inside. Before she went through, a car on the other side of the road pulled up and watched her. A large man wearing a pair of black sunglasses and a trench coat got out. He watched her as she went inside, once she was inside he pulled a mobile phone from inside his coat pocket. Dialing it he answered.

"Boss this is Powerhouse, I've managed to locate Stacey Roberts aka The Green Girl. What are my orders?"

For a second there was no answer, then a man's voice was heard. "I don't want you to engage her yet, just follow her and remain unseen if you can Powerhouse?"

Powerhouse smiled. "Understood boss."

Before he was about to hang up the man spoke again. "Once you engage her, Powerhouse. Bring her to me alive and uninjured, it's time that me and Miss Roberts had a chat."

Powerhouse hung up and returned to the car waiting for the right moment to strike.

CHAPTER SEVEN

Fashion Shoot

Green Girl was getting excited as she followed Jennifer thought the main door. They both went up a flight of stairs that had a red carpet laid out, once they had reached the top they both turned right and went thought into a large room. Inside were at least twenty or so female models, they all had different skin tones and colors. Jennifer looked at Stacey and smiled at her, Green Girl looked at her and smiled back, as they walked on thought to the back end of the room. Waiting for them both was the photographer.

"You are early," he said as he smiled at them both. "Are you ready for your close-up Miss Roberts?" he said as he pointed the camera towards her.

Stacey smiled at him back. "Ready whenever you are Mark," she giggled, as she looked at Jennifer who was smiling back at her.

"Great stuff girls, but I would like you to have change, would you both mind putting these on for me please?" Mark handed a black bra to Green Girl and pants, with a matching pair of long black opera gloves; Jennifer he handed a purple bra and pants, along with a pair of purple opera gloves.

As she was about to take them off, he gave her a look which puzzled her. "Besides wearing those Miss Williams, I would like you to get yourself to makeup, to be painted green."

As Green Girl and Jennifer made their way to the changing rooms, Jennifer looked over at her friend.

"That Mark creeps me out."

Green Girl could see that her friend was unhappy, so she put her hand on her shoulder. "Cheer up, Jen," she said in a friendly voice.

Jennifer looked at her friend with a hard stair. "It's ok to tell me to cheer up GG, Mark doesn't want you to be painted does he?" She let out a deep breath. "Look. I'm sorry/ I should not have said that like I did, it's just sometimes, I wish that had green skin like you."

Green Girl laughed, "Then I wouldn't be the only freak around here, would I?"

They both started laughing, as they made way into the changing rooms, to change into their clothes. It took them both just a few seconds to get themselves ready. Green Girl was the first to come out wearing what Mark had given her. Her long blonde hair was now tied back in a ponytail, on her feet she wore a pair of black high heeled shoes and on her face, she was wearing a pair of black sunglasses.

Green Girl waited for Jennifer as she was painted green. She hadn't been waiting too long before Jennifer made her way out of the changing room. Now painted from head to toe, in dark green body paint, she was wearing the clothes that Mark had given her, along with purple eye makeup and lipstick.

Green girl took off her sunglasses and smiled. "Gosh Jen," she said as she started laughing, "I never realized that you would look so sexy painted green?"

Jennifer then looked at her and laughed. "What about you?" she said checking Green Girl out. "You look amazing."

Both her and Jennifer made their way back to Mark, who had been getting the camera ready for the shoot. As they made their way to him, both he and the women were ready.

First, he took individual shots of them by their selves, next he took a few of them together and finial, he took a couple of them naked.

"Thanks very much ladies, I'll look forward to seeing you again for some over time."

As they were making their way down stairs Jennifer turned to Green Girl. "With a bit of luck, we both won't be working with that creep again. Why did he have us do that?"

Green girl looked at her friend. "You mean naked, don't you?" Jennifer nodded in agreement, Green Girl could tell that her friend wasn't ok with it. "Look Jen, this is just a job to you, but's it's a new life for me and I enjoy it."

Jennifer smiled at her friend. "I know that you enjoy this GG, but something tells me that something better will come up in your life."

Green Girl didn't answer her as she opened the main door and walked into the open. As she did this, Jennifer couldn't help but think that her friend's life was going to change. Stepping outside, Jennifer saw a large bald-headed man in a black trench coat, walking up to Green Girl.

CHAPTER EIGHT

Meeting with an old friend

Jennifer couldn't believe her eyes. Coming towards her friend was a monster of a man. He stopped right in front of her and talked loudly. He was dressed in a black trench coat which covered most of his body, on his face he was wearing a pair of black sunglasses.

"Hey, you," Jennifer said as he approached Green Girl. "Leave her alone right now or else!"

Green Girl looked at Jennifer. "It's ok, Jen," she said quietly. "This man knows my boyfriend Ben."

Jennifer couldn't believe what she had heard. "Ben, the boy who was undergoing the same experiments as you?"

Green Girl nodded her head, Powerhouse spoke. "Ben is very much alive and he would like to see you, Stacey."

Jennifer piped up. "Ok then, best not to keep him waiting then. I think that we should both go, don't you?"

Powerhouse gave Jennifer a dirty look. "The boss only wants to see Green Girl, not you Miss, as you are nothing to him."

Jennifer was going to say something to the giant, but Stacey butted in. "This woman is my friend. Please let her come with me."

Powerhouse didn't say anything but relented. "She can come, but you will have to explain your actions to the boss, he is not known for being patient."

He climbed into his car and instructed the two women to get in the back. He started the car's engine and slowly began to drive. The car drove past the estate and slowly passed town into the main city. During the journey, Stacey remembered how kind Ben had been, when they had first met and how encouraging he had been towards her, when she had told him that she was thinking about going to college.

"That's in the past now," she said to herself, as she saw the car coming near to, what looked like a penthouse. The car drove up to the building and stopped.

Powerhouse turned his head around. "Here we are, girls," he said in a gruff voice. "The boss is in that building."

He got out of the car and opened the back door, both Green Girl and Jennifer climbed out, soon as they were out of the car Powerhouse told them to follow him. Coming up to the building both women were impressed, as the front was made from solid green marble. They both made their way into the building and noticed that it was fully decorated. A marble staircase and water feature were in the middle of the hall and statures of lions and horses were on both sides.

Powerhouse passed them both. "The boss is on the top floor please follow me," he said as he began to climb the stairs.

Her and Jennifer began to climb the stairs. Stacey thought she could hear Ben's voice coming from the top room, it sounded to her like he was on the phone. As all three of them climbed towards the third floor of the house, they were met by two armed guards. Both men had black colored body armor and were armed with small handguns. They both waited at the top of the stairs to search them. After they had done this, both of the men went back down to the main entrance. Stacey and Jennifer followed Powerhouse who turned a corner to go down a corridor. They both followed turned and went through a door on their left. Going inside they saw a young man sitting at a desk with his back turned, standing next to him was another man. He was tall with a slim build, with dark blue eyes, short blonde colored hair. He was wearing a blue colored suit and it looked like he was waiting for Ben to finish.

As they entered the room Ben turned the chair around. "Stacey, is that you?" he said smiling as he ran over to meet her.

Stacey looked at him and smiled, Ben had gotten taller and he looked much older than he had, when they had first met. He now had a small blonde beard and short dirty blonde hair.

"Look at you, Ben," Stacey said as she threw her arms around him. "It's so good to see you. How have you been?"

Ben looked at her and smiled. "Not bad thank you," he said as he looked over his shoulder, at the man who had been standing next to the desk. "Frostbite, come over here and let me introduce you to my girlfriend." The man walked slowly over to them both, as he did he left a trail of what looked like ice. "Stacey," Ben then said smiling. "This is my business partner Frostbite." Frostbite gave her an icy look, Ben turned towards him. "Would it be possible if you and Powerhouse could give me and our guest time on our own, just so that I can fill her in on the details?" Frostbite turned towards the door and slowly walked out, who was followed by Powerhouse, leaving Ben, Stacey, and Jennifer. Ben slowly turned towards the two women and smiled. "Now then, where were we?"

CHAPTER NINE

Ben's offer

Stacey didn't say much as she looked at Ben. Ben was smiling at her showing a set of polished white teeth, as he came forward he stopped for a moment.

"Who is this?" He asked as he pointed to Jennifer.

Stacey smiled at him and then turned her head and smiled at her friend. "Ben," she said in a friendly voice. "This is my friend, Jennifer."

Ben smiled at them both and then raised one of his hands, for a brief moment.

Jennifer felt a sharp stabbing pain in her head. "Stacey," she said as she started to scream "What's happening? What's your boyfriend doing?"

For a few seconds, nothing was heard except Jennifer's screaming, then quiet. Jennifer stood there not moving. Stacey was worried and moved towards her friend.

"Jennifer, are you alright? Come on Jen, this isn't a joke." She then turned towards Ben, anger was in his eyes. "You son of a bitch," she said, as she moved towards him with lighting fast speed, with her fists raised. "What have you done to my friend?"

Ben dodged her attack and again raised one of his hands, like with what happened to Jennifer, Stacey could feel a sharp pain coming from inside her head. She began to understand Ben was a psychic. Ben let his hand drop and Stacey fell to the ground, he came towards her, dropping to one knee.

"Stacey," he said. "This is just a demonstration of my power." Stacey could feel her blood boiling inside her body. She could do nothing for herself or her friend. Ben continued, "I couldn't use my power on you, as it would have no effect. Instead I had to use your friend over there."

Stacey got back to her feet, as Ben moved over to where Jennifer was. She was now lying on the ground asleep. Stacey walked slowly over to her and put her knee down. She looked at Ben cold and hard.

"Will she be alright?" she asked him in an angry tone.

Ben looked at her and gave her a smile. "She should be waking up so time around, about now."

As soon as he said that, Jennifer's eyes flashed open. She looked around in a panic. "What happened? Where am I? Stacey, are you alright?"

Ben leaned over her. "Everything's ok Jennifer, your safe you're with friends," he said as he saw Stacey smiling at her.

She turned towards him. "For a minute there, you had me thinking that you'd killed her."

Ben's smile dropped, and he beckoned her and Jennifer into his office. There, both women sat down and watched as Ben demonstrated his powers again, this time levitating objects. They both watched as he then poured a bottle of water into a glass using his mind. Stacey looked impressed, as did her friend Jennifer.

Ben sat down in front of the two women. "This is what I've become Stacey," he said in a low voice. "I can use the power of my mind to control people, read their minds and to move and levitate objects."

Stacey gave him a puzzled look. "Why did you bring me all the way here then Ben? Wouldn't it have been a better display of your power if you had come to me?" Ben gave her a sadden look one that melted her heart. "Stacey. like yourself and so many of us who had been experimented on, I fear that we are being hunted."

"Hunted?" Stacey gasped as she held her hands up to her mouth. "By who or what Ben?"

Ben stood up and walked over slowly to where she sat. "By the militaries of the world, that's who." He then stopped for a moment to let things sink in and then continued. "You see Stacey after your escape from that medical center, the British government in all of their wisdom, had all of the worlds governments pool their resources to hunt down mutants like you and myself to be used in experiments." He then stopped to pause for a breath. "We were created by the government to be used for one thing and one thing alone, war. But it looks like they fear their own creations."

Stacey stood up and put her hand over one of Ben's shoulders, Ben looked into her dark green eyes and smiled. "So, this is because of me then?"

Ben gently touched her hand finding it smooth. "No," he said in a friendly voice. "People in power grow afraid when their power is challenged." He then paused. "When you escaped, the government realized that people of our abilities could not be used, unless our wills were controlled."

Stacey paused just to take in what Ben had said. "So, what you are saying, is, that we were meant to be only pawns of the government, to be used for war?"

Ben looked at her and smiled. "You were always very clever Stacey," he said as both him and Stacey looked at each other.

She then ran her hand down his face, the green skin of her hand felt warm and smooth on his cheek. Jennifer getting tired of seeing this walked out of the office, as the two of them began to kiss. Ben could taste something as he kissed her dark green lips. Stacey felt, like it had been a lifetime since they had both last kissed. For some reason with no thought she stopped. Ben looked at her, as he began to tell that something was on her mind.

"Stacey. are you alright?" he asked in a worried voice.

She turned her head to one side and then back to Ben. "I was just thinking well I know that this might sound stupid, but have you got a plan?"

Ben looked at her and smiled again. "I was thinking about starting up my own group. Would you be interested in joining me?"

Stacey looked at him and smiled. "Yes Ben, I would be very interested."

They then looked at each other and started kissing again, Ben then drew the blinds in his office.

CHAPTER TEN

The Hunt begins

It was a dark and storming night at a military base in Miami, standing tall looking for any sign of movement was LT John Watts, Watts was in his late forties with a clean military record. He was over six foot with dark black skin, he had a large scar on his right cheek and he was bald. As he was looking over to his left something caught his eye, it was a small military jeep with both of its headlight flashing, as he was looking at it one of the soldiers under his command came running up to him.

"Sir," he said as he stopped in front of him and took a deep breath, "Our guest has arrived and we are waiting for your instructions."

Watts smiled as he looked at the young soldiers face, "Very good soldier," he said as he began walking towards the car, "No further orders just yet until our guest is out of the jeep, then you and the rest of your unit will take her to the barracks," he then turned and gave the young man an angry glace, "Do I make myself clear?!"

The young man stood to attention, "Sir yes sir," he shouted as Watts turned back around and continued to walk towards the jeep.

It had stopped as he reached it and both of its headlights were off, he then made his way towards the back seats and began to open the door, from out the back seat stepped a scientist. She was in her late forties and had medium light colored brown hair, she was wearing a lab coat and had a pair of blue colored glasses on her face looked like that of a woman who was warm and friendly.

Watts looked at her and swallowed hard, "Welcome to Miami Dr Young, it is an honour for you to be-"

Dr. Young held up a hand to cut him off, "I'm not here to be welcomed by you or anyone else, Lt," she said in a sharp cold voice as she began walking with him, "I m here under orders from both the USA and British governments to hunt and collect the failed super soldiers that escape our private facility in the UK."

She stopped for a moment and Watts looked at her, "So it's true then, there are mutants all over the globe?"

Dr. Young gave his another icy stare as she began walking towards the entrance to the base, "Yes Lt," she said smiling, "I created the serum that transformed citizens into mutants, I was the one who was ordered by the military to use them as super soldiers for war."

She then paused as she went through a set of double door and then to the base, she then passed through a scanner, waiting for her on the other side were a group of soldiers, she looked at Watts as one of them began to scan her.

"You're all clear mama." he said smiling.

She then smiled and walked on followed by Watts, "So that was the Government's plan all along?" He said as he caught up with her, "Using unwilling tests to be transformed and converted into folder for war?"

Dr Young stopped again, "Rhese test subjects could have revolutionized the battlefield saving lives and preventing deaths, are you telling me Lt that innocent lives aren't worth saving?"

Watts stepped back from her, "You know as well as I do Doc," he said as he came forward, "War doesn't care whether you are a solder, a civilians or a child there will always be innocents who will loss their lives."

Dr. Young's face dropped as she listened to what the LT said, "I suppose you are right." She said as they carried on walking towards a set of double doors, "but I still need your help to track these mutants down."

Watts held a door open for her and let her walk thought, "What help do you want from me and how can I be of assistant?"

She then waited for him on the other side to catch up, as he was coming towards her she pulled something out from her pocket, it looked like a color photo of a young woman. She had long blonde hair and was of a slim build, she looked normal apart from the fact that she had green colored skin.

"Who is this girl?" Watts asked with a puzzled look on his face, Dr. Young smiled,

"That is my first test subject Lt, her name is Stacey Roberts and I believe that she is in Miami somewhere." Watts paused for a moment as he looked over the photo a smile began to appear over his face,

"I know of this girl," he paused again looking over the photo, "Or at least I know someone who looks very much like her I can't tell."

Dr. Young eyed him for a moment and then laugh, "Well then Lt. you had better start talking, command wants us to find her and place her and those like her under arrest."

Watts looked at her and smiled, "Don't worry yourself Doc, me and my men will find her I promise you that for sure."

As he was saying this his mobile phone rang, pulling in out of his pocket he answered it, "Watts. Yes, there has being a sighting of Stacey Roberts and you have a witness."

Dr Young listened patiently and with excitement as she began rubbing both of her hands together, once Watts finished on the phone he saw Dr Young's face light up. He looked at her as she was smiling.

"You look pleased." He said as he started to smile.

"Your men have just made it easy for us both, Lt," she said as she started laughing,

Watts looked at her and started laughing, "I have put a request in from command to question this witness about what she saw and where our friend is."

Dr Young then stopped and looked at Watts, "What is the witness's name?"

Watts gave her a slight smile, "Jennifer Williams." he said as they both carried on walking towards the barracks laughing as they went.

CHAPTER ELEVEN

Stacey's Nightmare

It was getting late as Stacey was getting ready for bed, she had been with Ben all day since then he had shown her around the penthouse. Ben had pieces are artwork that was worth quite a bit of money antique furniture and bookshelves full of classical novels, Ben's main goal was to help and create a safe haven for all mutants all over the world starting with the USA. As she was making her way to the bathroom coming up the stairs Stacey looked at a photo that was hanging up on a wall, it was of three young boys, one of them was wearing glasses and looked like Ben. She smiled as she looked at it and began to think to herself that Ben reminded her of what she had been like all those years ago before their transformation, she then quickly made her way up to the top of the stairs and up to the bathroom. Once she had reached the top she turned right and made her way to the end of the corridor where the bathroom was situated, gently she opened the door and slipped in closing the door gently behind her, inside she was surprised at what she saw. There was a wet room with a walk in shower on a side in a corner a way from the shower was a small cabernet with a large collection of aftershaves, above the cabernet was a mirror it's edges painted with gold leaf Stacey came forward and began to look at herself.

"Hello sexy," she said out loud as she started posing, "Does Ben know that you are here?" She said as she slowly stared to strip off to her black colored bra and underwear, as she did this she noticed something strange, her eyes normally a dark green color were beginning to change color from dark green to light blue, she then turned away thinking that she was seeing things. As she looked again she noticed that they were dark green.

"That's funny," she said to herself as she put her dirty clothes into a washing up basket, "I could have sworn that my eyes have changed color, maybe I'm tired."

She then came out of the bathroom and switched the light off, then she made her way towards Ben's master bedroom which was the first room on the left, as she went thought she turned the door handle and slowly opened the door. She stepped thought and again was surprised to find how big the room was, it was decorated with fur carpets on the floor priceless pieces of artwork hung on the walls, in one corner of the room was a king sized double bed with red coloured silk sheets, at the end of the room there was a balcony with a table and chairs outside sitting down on one of the chairs with a small glass of whiskey in one hand and a lit cigar in another was Ben his back was turned.

Before she stepped outside he felt her presents and turned slowly to face her, "Stacey," he said with a smile on his face, "So nice of you to except my offer of staying with me tonight."

Stacey smiled back at him, "Please help yourself to a glass and join me, won't you?"

By the table and chair, there was a small drinks cabernet, Stacey slowly went up to it and noticed that there was already a bottle of gin and a small bottle of tonic water out along with a glass, she began to pour herself one slowly and then went and sat by her boyfriend Ben. Ben slowly put his arm around her and felt the warmth of her naked green skin next to his, for the moment he had just a plain black dressing grown on and a pair of boxer shorts, Stacey looked into his eyes and smiled.

"Yu know Ben," she said in a soft voice, Wwhen I escaped from that medical center I didn't know whether or not I would ever see you again."

Ben turned his head around to face her and looked deep into her dark green eyes.

"Yhat day Stacey," he said as he let out a deep breath, "Not many people got out of that place alive."

Stacey looked at him with a look of shock on her face, "What do you me, Ben?" She asked in a voice that sounded afraid, Ben walked slowly over to the balcony and looked down.

"After you have been taken in to that lab one of the lads that I was with died,"

Stacey came over to him and put one of her hands over his, "I'm sorry that you had to witness that. Were you close to him?"

Ben looked at her and couldn't take his eyes off her.

"Yes," he said letting out another deep breath, "It was hard in there not having any family members with you so I all tried to be supportive to the others."

Stacey could remember that Ben had always been there for her and some of the other members. She then looked at him as she ran one of her green hands down his face.

"Tou shouldn't feel guilty about what happened Ben," she said her voice again was warm and friendly, "You were not responsible for your friends' death Dr. Young was."

Ben then turned his head towards the balcony again and took a sip of his whiskey then taking a drag on the cigar he put the glass down, he then lent over the balcony and turned again to Stacey.

"That's why I'm trying to set this group up just to give mutants a safe haven." He then picked up his glass and quickly downed the whiskey,

"Look it's getting late." He said as he slowly made his way towards the bed, "I'm off to bed now babe, come join me when you are ready."

As he made his way passed her he gave her a kiss on her cheek, Stacey took a small slip of gin and put the glass down back on the cabinet, she then followed Ben who was now in his pair of boxer shorts, Stacey's eyes nearly popped out of her head as she saw Ben's naked body. Nearly all of it was ribbed with muscle, Ben just laid there with his eyes shut, Stacey then threw herself onto the bed and onto him. Ben aware that she was about to do this on him let her, as she fell on top of him Ben opened his eyes, he then gently grabbed her and began kissing her passionately. Then both of them fell asleep in each others arms, Stacey had both her head and her hand on Ben's naked chest, as she was sleeping she began to dream. She was running through a wood in the dark, as she was running she came to a dead end with no way out, she then turned around to face whatever she was running away from and then she noticed something terrible. Looking at both of her hands she noticed that there were now pale white in colour, to make matters worse she noticed that her vision was now blurred she closed her eyes thinking that it would all go away. Then from out of nowhere she felt a hand tighten around her neck, she opened her eyes and found that it belonged to a large green-skinned woman, she was tall and had a slim build but unlike Stacey she had long black coloured hair and dark green coloured skin, as she tighten her grip around her neck Stacey began to scream. She then found herself sat up in bed covered in sweat, Stacey then lifted both of her arms up only to find that they were still green.

"Just a dream," she said to herself as she laid back down and closed her eyes, "Just a stupid dream." she told herself as she turned over onto her side and went back to sleep.

CHAPTER TWELVE

Jennifer's betrayal

It was getting light now as Jennifer woke up in her cell that she had been kept in overnight since her arrest, she had been lying down on the small mattress on the cell floor, as she was getting up she heard footsteps coming from outside her cell. Without warning the door opened and in walked a woman followed by a man, Jennifer eyed them both up as they walking into her cell and stopped to look at her.

"Are you, Jennifer Williams?" The woman asked her in a warm friendly voice.

Jennifer stood up and looked at the woman, to her she looked like a doctor or a scientist, "I am, miss." she said in a low voice.

The woman smiled and her face looked friendly, "My name is Dr. Sarah Young, Jennifer and this is Lt John Watts." she then paused as she slowly came forward, "Qe both believe that you have some information that could help us track down a very dangerous woman would you be willing to cooperate with us?"

Jennifer smiled as she knew who Dr. Young was talking about.

"You mean Stacey Roberts. don't you?" She said smiling,.

Lt Watts stepped forward, "Yes Jennifer, and we would be willing to do anything to reward you only if you provide us with information that would lead to her capture."

Jennifer then stood between them and said nothing as she began thinking what she would like. Then as she looked at Dr. Young something came over her.

"You are the creator of that serum aren't you Doctor, the one that was used on Stacey?"

Dr. Young pushed passed Lt Watts and started to laugh. "What a clever young woman you are Jennifer, yes I was the one who created the super soldier serum that was used on Stacey." she then paused and looked at the young woman, "Why do you want to become like Stacey is now?"

Jennifer gave her an icy cold look, "Is there anything wrong wanting to become like something she is?" She said as she became angry. "Since that bitch has known me she has always been the center of attention and now I want my share,"

Dr. Young and Lt Watts both looked at each other and smiled. "At last," Dr Young said to herself, "After all these long years we have got a willing test subject."

She then came forward and put her hand on Jennifer's shoulder. "Stacey stole something important from you didn't she?"

Jennifer look up at her tears were in her eyes as she did. "She stole a lot of things from me Doctor, my life my work. even some of my boyfriends, I just want to get even with her now."

Dr. Young smiled as she heard this, "And you will my dear, we just need that information that you have on her, remember you help us and I will do my best to help you."

Jennifer looked at her and smiled, "OK then, here is what I know at the moment. Stacey is working with her boyfriend Ben Fox."

As she said that name Watts grew interested, "Wait. did you say Fox?"

Jennifer looked at him and smiled, "I did Lt. why?"

Watts came forward to her and smiled, "Fox is on one of our most wanted mutants lists for acts of terrorism and violence against non-mutants," he then took a step back and smiled, "You have just made both mine and Dr. Young jobs easier kid/"

Jennifer smiled at them both, "So I can get that reward that you promised me?"

Dr. Young put her hand out and Jennifer took it, "If you wish to become like your friend then you will need to be stronger," she said as she took her out of the cell and down a corridor, "I can give you a stronger dose of the serum that Stacey received, but we are going to have to test you first."

Jennifer looked up at her and smiled, "I'll take any chance that you've got Dr anything to take that bitch and her boyfriend down."

Dr. Young started laughing, "Jennifer. once you have taken this serum you can have your revenge on both of those two." She then took her into a private room and locked the door from the inside cutting them both off.

CHAPTER THIRTEEN

The Attack

It was a warm midday as Stacey was lying on a sunbed by a pool at the back of the penthouse, she was wearing a purple bikini and a pair of sunglasses, next to the bed was a table with a large glass that was filled with alcohol.

Stacey reached over and took a sip from the glass, "Awww," she said to herself as she started to relax, "This is the life."

As she was saying this Ben came over to her, Stacey let her sunglasses drop over her face and looked at him as he passed by.

"Hey there handsome," she said in a sexy voice, "Fancy sitting by me to soak up some sun?"

Ben looked at her and smiled, "Sure Stacey, why not?" he said as grabbed a spare sun bed and lay beside her.

As he was lying beside her Stacey grabbed his hand and began smiling at him.

"Ben," she said in a soft voice, "Thank you for giving me this chance to be with you."

Ben looked at her and smiled back, "You are very welcome Stacey." he said as he gave he a smile back.

No sooner had they done this then they both went to kiss each other, without warning and for no reason at all Ben stood up. Stacey took his hand and looked up at him,

"What's wrong, Ben?" She asked in a worried voice,

Ben gave her a worried look of his own, "I'm not sure." he said as he grabbed a pair of jeans from the sunbed where he had been lying.

He then looked at her with a face that was afraid, "I don't know what it is Stacey, but I can sense that something is off."

As he was getting up Ben called out to one of his private security guards, the young man came running over to Ben, like the guards who had first searched her and Jennifer the young man was wearing a black armored vest with a handgun in a holster at his side. He was armed with a large AK47 machine gun, Stacey could hear Ben shouting orders and she grew afraid after the young guard left him Ben returned back to were Stacey was, as soon as she saw him returning she got up from the sunbed and made her way towards him. By the look on his face Stacey saw that Ben was angry.

"Is everything all right?" She asked him as he went passed her to the sun bed where he had been lying, "Ben what's wrong?" Stacey said as she sat beside him putting one of her arms across his waist.

Ben looked at her and for the first time in her life Stacey knew that he was afraid.

"They have found us, Stacey." He said in a worried voice.

Stacey gave him a puzzled look, "They, who are they? Ben what the hell are you talking about?" As she said this there was a loud bang followed by a shower of broken glass.

Quickly Ben grabbed Stacey and used his psychic powers to form a protective shield around them both, as he did this the glass just harmlessly bounced off, from inside the shield both of them heard gunfire followed by shouting. Once the shield had died Ben grabbed Stacey by the hand and dragged her away.

"Our best chance to escape is up to the roof, where we can get a helicopter and fly out of here."

Stacey then looked at him, "What about the others Ben, will they be alright?"

Ben gave her a faint smile, "I ordered my men to get Frostbite, Powerhouse, Flamethrower, and Mist out before they come back for us."

They were both running inside the house towards the stairs as Ben was saying this,

"We should be OK once we get to the sta-." His words were cut short standing in front of them armed were a full platoon of soldiers, they have guns aimed at them both, Ben looked at Stacey, "Get down, both of you or we will open fire!" Shouted one of the soldiers at the front.

Ben leaving Stacey walked slowly forward, "Now now," he said in a mild voice, "There is no need for violence," he said as he waved one of his hands.

Just then one of the soldiers went flying as Ben sent out a wave of psychic energy at him, seeing this the other soldiers began to open fire, Ben just caught the bullets in mid-air and let them drop harmlessly to the ground. Seeing how powerful he was the others dropped their weapons and started running towards the door screaming leaving they squad mate on the ground, Ben and Stacey slowly went up to the man.

Stacey looked at him and then Ben. "Is he dead Ben did you kill him?"

Ben looked at her puzzled,

"He's not dead, Stacey just stunned, if I wanted to kill him I could have choked him with a mere thought."

She then looked at him and smiled, "You still haven't changed." she said as she kissed him on his cheek, "you are still that sweet young man who I fell in love with all those years ago."

Ben started to laugh, as he gently pressed his hand on the young man's head, he then closed his eyes and started to concentrate, Stacey seeing this didn't say anything as she knew that Ben had the ability to read minds. It lasted only a few minutes and when it was over Ben placed the young man down gently, Stacey walked slowly up to him and place one of her hands on one of his shoulders,

"What did you learn and is that man going to be OK?" Ben got back up and looked at her, "That man will be fine as for us I don't know what will happen."

Stacey gave him a puzzled look, "What do you mean Ben?"

"He means me," a voice shouted coming from the door behind them, slowly turning her head to face the voices owner Stacey had a nasty surprise, standing at the main entrance wearing a white tank top and a pair of jeans and black boots was Jennifer, she looked the same as she had before she had decided to leave the penthouse and Stacey but they had been changed. Jennifer was well over six foot, she had long lose jet black coloured hair and her skin colour was now a dark green colour, Stacey could tell by the look on her face that she was angry.

"Hello Stacey," she said as she slowly was walking towards both her and Ben, "Do you like my new look?" She said in an angry tone, "I sure hope that you do because I will be the last person that you and your boyfriend see."

Both Stacey and Ben began to look at each other as there was nowhere to run or hide.

CHAPTER FOURTEEN

Stacey VS Jennifer

Ben and Stacey looked at other another as Jennifer was almost on top of them, as she almost reached her Stacey came forward.

"Jennifer," she said in a friendly voice as she tried to get her away from both her and Ben, "Please don't do this, we are friends after all, aren't we?"

For a brief moment Jennifer stood still then she started to laugh, "Friends, friends?!" she roared, "Why would I want to be friends with you after what you have done to me bitch?"

Stacey stepped a few paces back from her as she said it, she could feel herself getting upset and angry, Jennifer then continued to mock her. "You stole everything from me, you green-skinned bitch, but now I have even more power than you and I also have become more attractive than you."

As she continued saying these word she didn't notice Stacey running towards her with one of her fists out, as Stacey hit her and Jennifer went flying into the water feature near the entrance to the penthouse, as she hit it, it smashed into pieces leaving nothing but dust and rubble. Stacey then ran over to where the water feature had been and found Jennifer lying on the ground covered in small cuts and brushes her jeans and the tank top she had been wearing were now ripped, as she was leaning over her Jennifer raised her hand and grabbed her by her neck.

"You stupid green bitch," she mocked. "Look what you have done."

As she raised her hand to hit her Stacey used her right hand and clenched it into a fist, she then hit her former friend in the stomach winding her, as Jennifer let go of her she held her stomach in pain and cried, once Stacey was free and began to use her nails as weapons. She came slowly up to her former friend and slashed her across her face, green blood started pouring out from the cuts as Jennifer tried to hold Stacey back, as she did this she stumbled back where the water feature had been and tripped over some of the rubble. Stacey held back as she saw her friend falling to the ground, with a sickening crack Jennifer's head hit the a lose stone and hit the marble floor not moving, Stacey didn't go up to her this time but she noticed that Ben did. Ben put his hand on her head and began to read her mind, Stacey walked up slowly as he was doing this and looked at him, once he had finished he looked at her.

"Stacey," he said in a worried voice, "I've got some bad news for you."

Stacey looked at him and her head was down, she had felt awful as she had turned on her former friend like that.

"What's the news. babe?" She asked him as she slowly backed away from Jennifer's body.

"Jennifer wasn't under any sort of mind control. That's my gift, she was acting out because she was jealous."

Stacey looked at him and started laughing, "Jealous? Get real, Ben," she said as saw that Ben looked worried, "What had that bitch got to be jealous of with me?"

Ben looked at her and took a deep breath, "Everything Stacey, you were far more intelligent than her, far more attractive and far more popular than she could ever wish to be."

Stacey- looked at Ben and for a moment said nothing, then she started crying, "Yes I think that you are right and she was too?" She ran up to Ben and threw her into his arms as she cried on his shoulder, "I took a lot of things from her Sean and now I've taken her life."

Ben gently made her feel better as he said to her, "Stacey, she attacked you. It was either you or her, you can't blame yourself for Jennifer's death."

As he was saying this he started gently rubbing her back with one of his hands. He could feel how smooth her green skin was and with his other hand he held it at the back of her head. he then let go and they looked at each other.

"Come on, Stacey," he said in a friendly voice. "Dry those beautiful dark green eyes of yours and come upstairs to me I've got something a want to share with you."

After he said this Ben disappeared upstairs and left Stacey looking over Jennifer's body, as Stacey looked at her she noticed something odd, all of the cuts and all of the brushes that she had been inflicted hadn't healed, was this was Sean wanted to talk to her about or was it something else perhaps about her past? As she was waiting around she noticed that there was a bright blue mist near her, it seemed to settle next to her, without warning there was a bright blue flash. Stacey cover and closed both of her eyes, when she opened them again she was surprised to see that it was Mist standing next to her. Mist had teal colored blue skin and medium-long dark brown hair, she was wearing a pair of leather trousers and a black leather bra, on her hands she had a pair of black leather gloves. Unlike Stacey who had super speed, super healing and strength Mist's had the power to teleport long distances, looking at Stacey Mist smiled at her.

"What up. Green Girl? You and the boss been busy?" She asked in an Australian accent, she then looked over to Jennifer who's body hadn't been removed, "Who is that and are you responsible?" She asked,

Stacey looked at her, "It was an accident Mist, Ben can explain what happened."

Mist gently put one of her gloved hands on Stacey's shoulders. "I can see from the look in your face GG that you are telling me the truth, don't worry I'll get Powerhouse to shift the body."

Stacey gave her a friendly smiled, "Thank you, but I think Ben wants to keep it. Speaking of Ben he wants to see me, I better not keep him waiting,"

Stacey then slowly walked away from the main reception and up the stairs, what Ben wanted she would soon find out.

CHAPTER FIFTEEN

Another Green Girl

It was late at the army's base as John made her way towards Doctor. Young's office, he had recently been informed of his squad's failed mission and Jennifer's death at the hands of Stacey, as he passed thought the door to Sarah's office he noticed something strange. Sarah's office door was open.

"That's funny," John said to himself as he walked slowly up to the open door to look inside, "Dr. Young usually keeps this door closed I wonder if everything's OK."

As he peered inside he noticed that Dr. Young wasn't at her desk, that were very odd since Dr. Young had come to the base she very rarely left her office door open, Lt Watts decided to investigate further. As he was walking into the office he heard a familiar voice coming from behind.

"Excuse me Lieutenant," it said sharply. "But what do you think you are doing by walking into my office uninvited?"

John turned his head around and met face to face with Dr. Young,

"Doctor," he said in an alarmed voice, "I am sorry for the rude intrusion when I saw that the door was open I though that something was wrong."

Dr. Young wasn't listening as she went pass him and walked into her office, once she was in he heard her voice/ "You can come in now Lieutenant, I want to have words with you."

Lt Watts then walked slowly into the open office and saw that Dr. Young was now sat at her desk, she was sitting behind an Apple Mac laptop typing, behind her was a large open window that looked out over to the base's airfield. John sat down on a spare chair and waited until she had finished before he said anything to her, once she had finished typing she shut the laptop down and folded, she then looked at the Lt. John could tell from the look on her face that she was angry about something and he bet that he knew what it was.

"Lt John Watts," she said in an angry voice, "The reason why I wanted a word with you is because I have heard from command that during the attack on Fox's penthouse some of your men deserted is this true?"

John's face dropped and he looked down as if he was still a young child,

"It is true, Doctor," he said as he began to put his together.

Dr. Young that slammed her hand down in a fist onto the table causing the lieutenant to near jump out of his skin.

"I have heard also that we lost Jennifer to that freak, Stacey. I hope that you can explain this to command."

The lieutenant didn't say anything he just looked at her with his head down as if he had buried it in a sand pit, Dr. Young then stood up and walked over to a large fish tank at the side of the room, she then turned to the lieutenant and smiled as she walked back to her desk. The lieutenant stayed still as she sat back down, as she sat down Watts heard her laughing,

"What's so funny Sarah?" He asked in a puzzled voice/

"John," came her reply, "I should have known that Jennifer couldn't have taken on Stacey, after all, she was only just a model with no real combat experience."

Watts face dropped at her change of personalities, he didn't say anything as he didn't want her to blame him for anything else that might have gone wrong, she then slowly took her pair of glasses off and gently put them down onto her desk.

"John," she said and her voice now was clarm and friendly, "Command and I have been thinking to get back at both Fox and Roberts we need to use someone who has a lot of combat experience someone who knows the battlefield someone like our own what do you think?"

John looked at her and smiled, "Are you saying that we need to experiment on our own solder's?"

Dr. Young's smiled at him as she stood up again only this time she walked slowly over to where he was sitting.

"Yes John," she said as she kissed him lightly on his cheek, John slowly back away as he hated being so close to her, "But that serum that you gave that girl Jennifer was ineffective, how can you be sure that it won't be the same to our own people?"

Sarah sat herself down on his lap and smiled as she began to undo the buttons on his uniform. "that serum that I gave that hot-headed bitch was a prototype that's the reason why she lost that battle and ended up losing her life."

John then turned his head towards her, "So that Stacey got the full works then when she got injected?"

Sarah gave him another smile as she tossed his shirt over her desk.

"That is what makes that Stacey so special John," she said as she was now looking at the lieutenant's bare chest, it was covered by scars both old and new. John looked at her as she had one of her hands around his waist.

He then grabbed it and looked at her and smiled, "I take it that you have got more of this serum that you used on Roberts then?"

She then softly laughed, "Of course I do, John! What a stupid question."

John didn't say anything until she stood up, she then went back over to her desk and turned her laptop back on.

See her do this John sat down and waited patiently, her then heard the printer at the far side of the room. "Do you have an idea of which of our men to use for your science project?"

Hearing this Sarah stood up and went over to the printer, looking over at her Watts could see that she had a sheet of paper in her hand, she then came over and handed him the paper. Watts had a look at it on the front was a headshot of a young female soldier, she had medium red coloured hair and tanned coloured skin underneath the photo was the young woman name age and profile, Sarah sat back down at her desk and looked over at John smiling.

"Well. what do you think of her then John?" She asked him eager to hear what he had to say.

John looked at the photo again and smiled, "Her name is Trisha Morgan, it says here that she served in the army since she was 21 years of age," he then stopped and paused for a moment, "Are you sure about this, Sarah? Using someone of great value like this young woman in your experiments?"

"John," she say as she stood up again and make her way towards him, "This order came from command not me."

She then paused as she looked over at Trisha's photo, "if command has given this order then they must be running out of options."

She then turned her head towards John, "Please continue as I am interested to learn more about this girl."

John then slowly found where he was up to, "In 2007 she served both US and British forces in Iraq, during the war she was taken prisoner but later rescued by a joined unit of Navy Seals and British special forces, she is only 32 years of age."

arah looked at John eager to get his thought, "Well," she said in an impatient tone, "What do you think of her?"

John looked at her and smiled, "I haven't had the honour of working with her, but I am sure with her combat experience both of those freaks won't stand a chance."

Sarah then turned away from John and sat back down at her desk,

"Good, it's settled then, I'll give command a call and they can arrange Morgan to come here for a medical, then afterward I will inject the serum and we can have our very own loyal super soldier." John then got up and was about to go when Sarah got up, she then threw her arms around him and stared kiss him, John didn't really know what to do but play along.

CHAPTER SIXTEEN

A New Safe House

It was getting late in the afternoon as Stacey made her way up the stairs to Ben since the attack the whole of the penthouse had be put on red alert, Powerhouse had removed Jennifer's body and Mist had taken the solder that Ben had stunned away to be questioned. Stacey was nearing the top of the stairs when she heard Ben shouting at someone, she could tell what he was saying but it sounded like he was angry, just as she reached the top of the stair she saw something strange, an odd man came out from behind a door. He was about five foot eight in height, had short black hair and brown colored eyes, he also had bags underneath them, he passed Stacey and went into the office, as he did this Stacey thought that she could see him shift forms into someone else. She then went through the door and into the office herself there she saw Ben and Frostbite, they both looked like they were having a heated argument with one another, Stacey drew closer and listened.

"Ben." Frostbite coldly said in a Russian accent, "When are you going to open your eyes to the truth, that girlfriend of yours brought those hunters here?"

Ben grew angry as he heard this, "Do not forget Sergei, that I am the leader of this organization, not you, I hold the cards around here."

Frostbite started laughing, "You might be our leader Ben, but you are losing control right now under your very nose your so call followers are leaving."

Before Ben could say anything else to Frostbite he noticed the odd man coming forward, he turned his head towards Sergei.

"We will talk more Sergei, in the meantime, I've got other business to sort out."

Frostbite left the office in a huff and didn't even say any more to him. Once Frostbite had left Ben turned to face his new guest.

"Welcome Shifter I trust that you have news for me?"

The man then morphed back into the form that Stacey had seen he had taken on the stairs, he looked at Ben and smiled, "I do indeed Ben," he said in an Irish accent, "It looks like those pigs that attacked this place are onto you and that girlfriend of yours."

Ben slowly came forward, "Do you have an idea whom we are dealing with Shamus?" He asked in a worried sort of voice.

Shamus put a hand inside one of the pockets of the jacket that he was wearing and pulled out a cigar, "It'll be either the military or those other pigs the Outcasts."

Ben seemed pleased about what he heard, "So Shamus if the military is involved then that means our old friend John Watts could be behind this attack then?"

Shamus nodded, "Normally I wouldn't agree with anything that Frostbite said, but don't you think that you are putting yourself in danger with that girl?"

Ben face looked angry as he went over to the window and looked out at the city.

"What you have me do Shamus?" He said as he clenched one of his hands into a fist, "Turn her over to the military to be used in their sick experiments?"

Shamus came up to Ben and put a hand on his shoulder. "What about you and her taking a little holiday, you have that penthouse in New York City what about going there?"

Ben smiled at him, "What an excellent idea, Shifter. I'll make preparations right away thank you."

Shamus nodded and went out of the office, as he was about to leave he heard Ben's voice shouting behind him, "Tell Stacey that I am ready to see her right away."

Shamus nodded as he left, as he was passing through the door he noticed Stacey on the other side.

"Well, hello there Miss," he said in a friendly voice, "You must be Stacey, Ben's girlfriend."

Stacey smiled, "I am well I like calling myself Green Girl now. Shamus then smiled at her and laughed. Stacey then started laughing herself, "I am sorry, did I catch your name?" She said smiling.

"My names Shamus, but everyone around here just calls me Shifter." Stacey didn't admit to seeing him change.

"Why Shifter?" She asked looking puzzled.

Shifter looked at him smiling still, "Allow me to demonstrate" He said as he started twisting and turning his body around in odd directions.

As he was doing this he body began to take on another shape that of a female. Stacey was amazed for right in front of her was Shamus except he had morphed himself into her.

"Well. what do you think?" He said as he used her voice, "pretty cool or what?"

Stacey smiled at him, Shamus nodded his head.

"By the way before I forget," he said, "Ben wants to talk with you."

Saying this he ran down the stairs leaving Stacey to face her boyfriend,

"I don't like this now," she said to herself as she forced herself to go into the office and face Ben. "What if he turns me over to the military?" She thought to herself, "No, I'm not going anyway without a fight."

CHAPTER SEVENTEEN

Stacey's choice

Stacey stormed through to the office she saw Ben standing by the window with his back turned, as she came up to face him he turned.

"Stacey, thank you for coming." Stacey looked at him and he could tell that she was angry with him, "Is everything OK?"

Stacey clenched one of her hands into a fist, "I heard everything from Frostbite Ben, and it sounds like he doesn't trust me."

Ben came forward to her and put his hand on one of her shoulders, "Stacey, Frostbite has issues with trusting people."

She looked at him, "But you trust me, don't you babe?" She said as she brushed her hands against his arm.

Ben looked at her and smiled faintly, "If I didn't trust you would I have invited you into my home and shared my bed with you?"

Stacey looked at him and then lowered her head,

"I'm sorry, Ben." she said as she became upset, "Going up against Jennifer has really affected me trusting or getting close to people myself."

Ben gently lifted her head up with his hand, "That is the military plan, Stacey. Using our own friends or even our own families against us."

Stacey looked at him and nodded her head. "Thank you, babe." She said as she reached out and kissed him on his cheek.

"I don't know what I would do without you." Ben looked at her and kissed her hand, "I love you, Stacey, that why I am helping you but I want to know what do you want me to do for you now?"

Stacey looked at him with a puzzled look on her face, "I overheard you mention something about another penthouse somewhere in New York, is that right?"

Ben smiled at her, "No one else knows about it apart from Frostbite and myself and now you."

Stacey looked at him and smiled, "If it's possible I would like to go there as long as it's safe."

Ben put his arms around her and held her tight, "Not many people are aware that the military doesn't bother with New York so for the time being it's far safer than here."

Stacey grew excited as she heard this she had never been to New York before, "When can we go, Ben?" She asked as Ben let her go and went over to his chair, he looked at her as she started jumping around the room like an excited child.

"I was thinking maybe tonight?" He said as he had he hand in a drawer and pulled out a cigar, Stacey's eyes lit up.

"Wonderful! I'll start packing in few things then." She said as she rushed out of the office and into the corridor.

Ben smiled to himself as he lit the cigar and started leaning in the chair as he was smoking it, at the end of the day all he wanted was to keep Stacey safe, also when it came down to it she would be the one who could win the war not him. As he sat back he was aware that Mist had entered the room, she slowly walked up in front of him and put one of her gloved hands on his chest.

"Ben," she said in a soft and caring voice, "Are you, alright love?"

Ben looked at her and smiled faintly, "I'm OK Laura just a bit worried."

Mist slowly came forward to him and sat in between his legs, "Look, Ben, don't get worried about leaving us behind, you should know that we will take good care of this place when you and GG are gone."

Ben smiled at him as they both closed in for a kiss, as they both did this Ben pulled away, Mist looked at him, "What's wrong? Why did you pull away like that? Aren't I attractive enough?"

Ben gently pushed her off his lap and looked at her, "I'm sorry Laura as attractive as you are I can't cheat on Stacey."

Mist gave him a hard look, "Why Ben? Is it because of my skin color? Because if it is I could always go green for you."

Ben looked at her, "No, it's not that, Laura. The fact is that I love Stacey not you, you are just a friend nothing else."

Hearing this Mist stormed out of the office, as she was about to leave she turned towards him, "You know what your problem is Ben you have allowed yourself to get too close to that girl, you are too focused on her and not enough on me or anyone else."

She stormed out leaving him alone, "Maybe she is right." Ben said to himself as he sat back in the chair, "Maybe I am too focused on Stacey, but that's my business no one else's."

He sat back and relaxed closing his eyes and using his mind to guide the cigar into the ashtray that he kept in a draw on his desk when both him and Stacey were in New York things would become better for them.

CHAPTER EIGHTEEN

Trisha Morgan

It was early evening as Lt John Watts and Dr. Sarah Young were waiting outside their barracks for Trisha to arrive, since her stay Sarah had developed feelings for John, however, John didn't feel the same for her, for some odd reason he was afraid of her not because of her intelligence but there was something else about her. As they were waiting Sarah grabbed his hand, John turned his head to her as he did this she smiled at him.

"Something bothering you isn't it John?" She asked in a soft voice, John looked at her puzzled.

"Nothing bothering me, Sarah," he said as he turned his head away from her and looked at the coastline in front of the base.

Sarah then let go of his hand and stepped in front of his view.

"There is something on your mind that you are not telling me." She said in an angry voice, "Come on now John, tell me!"

John looked at her and then turned his head to the side, "I've just been thinking that's all, what if this plan of yours goes sour, then what do we do?"

The smile on her face faded as she heard him say that, "How will it go sour John?" She asked him in an angry voice, he then turned his head towards her.

"I don't have to remind you Sarah, that we worked with that former friend of Ms. Roberts and she let us down by getting herself killed."

Sarah laughed as she heard this. "John," she said in a tone that sounded like she was mocking him, "That foolish girl was consumed by anger and rage. She thought about nothing except revenge on Stacey, Trisha, on the other hand, is a professional soldier and has more battlefield experience than either those other two."

She then paused as she saw something heading toward the base. It was a small military helicopter that had been painted yellow, on both sides on the front there were two large machine gun barrels, at the front, there was an open cockpit, both John and Sarah rushed as the helicopter landed a few yards from the base. As they both made their way towards it they noticed that the first person to get out of the vehicle was the pilot, from the look of him he looked young, he was wearing a red jumpsuit and a helmet on his feet he wore a pair of large black colored boots. As they both came towards him they noticed that he was smiling.

"Hello Lieutenant, hello ma'am." he said in a friendly southern American voice, "I hope ya both doing well?"

John gave him a hard look and smiled, "We are both doing well boy, where is private Morgan is she OK?"

The young man smiled as he slowly turned away from the chopper and spat.

"She's out in the back sir," he said as he turned his head back to face the Lt. John smiled at him and saluted

"We'll take from here, report back to base for debriefing solder."

The young pilot saluted back, "Roger that sir, tenfold."

He then slowly turned and walked towards the barracks leaving the helicopter, John and Sarah, they both made their way to the rear of the chopper, John found a slot and slowly opened the passengers' door. Sitting down on a long green leather seat was Trisha, her red colored hair was in a short ponytail and she was wearing a green and brown army uniform, she had been asleep for most of the way but was now wide awake. Seeing both Lt Watts and Dr. Young she stood up and saluted.

"Ms. Morgan," Dr. Young said in a warm voice, "Welcome to our army base."

Trisha got out from the helicopter and stood tall and proud in front of them both.

"Thank you ma'am. It's an honor to have been selected for this program." she said in a Southern American accent.

"Please follow me to the barrack Morgan, we will get you processed there." John said as he placed a hand on her shoulder.

The three of them made their way slowly up to the barracks, as they were making their up Trisha grew excited.

"So Doctor," she said as she walked towards her, "What is this experiment that you want to perform on me?"

Sarah smiled at her, "It's not an experiment as such Trisha it's more of a serum."

Trisha smiled at her, "Sounds like something from one of those geeky SCFI films."

She then started laughing as they got near to the barracks before they went in Sarah put out one of her hands in front of Trisha.

"Before we go anywhere near the lab I need to do a medical with you if that's OK."

Trisha smiled, "Sure Doctor, what will that involve?"

Sarah back smiled at her, "Just a simple blood test that's all, you don't have to worry about it."

Trisha grew excited and smiled at her again, "Sounds great let's go for it."

Sarah took her by her arm and lead her inside, as she did this they both left John who now had lit up a cigar and started to smoke it.

CHAPTER NINETEEN

Leaving the Penthouse

It was five o clock in the morning as Ben and Stacey woke up, Stacey had her arm around his waist for the entire night, like they had before the night after she had arrived at the penthouse they both had sex only this time they hadn't been naked. She had been wearing a purple bra and pants whilst Ben had been wearing a pair of blue boxer shorts, as she woke up she noticed Ben on the other side of the bedroom, he was wearing a pair of casual stone-colored trousers a black colored shirt and a jacket. He looked over at her and smiled.

"Hey there sleeping beauty." he said to her as she slowly got up out of bed, she looked at him and smiled back.

"Very funny Ben." she said as she tried not to laugh at him, he then went over to the bed and held out his hand to her. "Come on Stacey. time to get up now as we don't want to be late."

Stacey let out a yawn and got to her feet, she then made her way to a large wardrobe that Ben had put in the middle of the room, as she went through it she couldn't make up her mind what it was that she wanted to wear. Finally, she came to the end and pulled out a pink colored tee shirt and a pair of blue skinnier jeans, she held them up to her waist and smiled, "Babe, what do you think of me in these?"

Ben smiled as he came over to her, "I think that you look hot babe." He said as he tried to hide a smile. "Lookmm I'll let you get ready so that we can go, ok hun?" he said as he made his way out of the room.

A few minutes Stacey came out, she was wearing the pink colored t-shirt and the jeans, she was also wearing a brown colored leather jacket and on her feet were a pair of high heeled black leather boots. As he was looking at her Ben's face dropped.

"Wow," he said in a surprised voice, "Looking good, babe."

Stacey looked at him and smiled showing him her polished white teeth.

"Thank you, babe." she said in a sexy voice, "Are we ready to go now?" She said as she took his hand, Ben's looked at her and nodded.

"I just had a call from the pilot upstairs, he's informed me that the helicopter's ready for take off."

They then both made their left onto the landing, after walking along the corridor they looked at an open doorway, they both walked through and found themselves standing at the bottom of a long staircase. They both looked at each other and smiled, they then let go of one another hands and raced up to the roof, at first Ben was in the lead his psychic powers giving him the edge that he needed, but then he noticed Stacey gaining speed at first she seemed to be holding back. As he turned his head around to her he could sense that the determination rushing through her like a storm, she then caught him up and passed him rushing up to the open door on the other side where the helipad was. It took Ben all his time to meet her at the top once he did he was exhausted, Stacey looked at him and smiled.

"Looks like I win today, Ben." She said as she raised both of her hands up in the air and cheered herself.

He smiled as he walked slowly up towards her and reached out to grabbed her by her waist, as he was about to do this he sensed someone behind him. Quickly turning around he came face to face with the pilot, he was a middle-aged man who was wearing a tight black uniform.

"Boss," he said as he smiled, "I am ready to take you and Ms. Roberts to New York now."

Ben looked at him and smiled, "Very good Jack, just give us both five minutes."

Jack nodded and made his way to the helicopter. As he was doing this Ben turned towards Stacey and smiled.

"Are you ready to leave here and come to New York with me?" He asked her as she was smiling back at him.

Stacey threw her arms around him and kiss him gently on his cheek, "Of course I'm ready Ben, I can't wait, babe."

They then took each other's hands and made they way to the helicopter, once they were there Ben threw open the passages door and both of them climbed inside, inside the helicopter was quite large in the passages area there was a large black leather seat. Both Ben and Stacey made themselves comfortable as Jack came round and closed the door.

"It's going to be good weather today boss."

He shouted over to Ben, "Are you both ready?" He asked in a friendly voice.

"We are Jack," Stacey shouted back at him turning to Ben as she said this and smiling.

Jack then slowly started the engine and the helicopter lifted slowly from the ground, Stacey turned towards the window and looked out. The penthouse was now only a small speck as with the other buildings, as she did this Ben gently put one of his hands on her shoulders, she turned and looked at him.

"It's OK," he said in a soft voice, "Don't worry about the penthouse we will go back as soon as it is safe to do so."

Hearing this she threw her arms around him and started kissing him madly, he closed both eyes as she did this and relaxed, he had predicted that once they arrived in New York they would both be safe. He had also predicted that his Florida penthouse would be also safe with the likes of Frostbite, Powerhouse, and Mist keeping watch/

"No need to worry, Ben." he said to himself as he gently place one of his hands over the back of Stacey's head, "All of us will be completely safe."

CHAPTER TWENTY

The New York Penthouse

Stacey couldn't believe her eyes when she the helicopter that they had been traveling in finally reached the penthouse in New York, it was a large building on top on a skyscraper, she looked at it as the helicopter began to land. As Jack opened the door to let both her and Ben out Stacey turned towards him and smiled.

"I can't wait to see what this penthouse is like Ben." She said as she started to undo the seat belt that she had to fasten around her waist, as both her and Ben climbed out then again took each other hands and started walking towards the penthouse before they could make a move Stacey heard Jack shouting.

"Excuse me, boss," he said in a worried sounding voice, "I've just received a message from the Mayor of New York, it seems like someone's got wind of your visit."

Ben looked at Jack with a puzzled look on his face.

"That's odd," he said to the pilot in a surprised voice. "I never informed Peter that I was coming. I wonder who has." As he was saying this the front doors to the penthouse opened and out walked a tall slim man, he had black colored skin and short silver colored hair, looking at him move towards Ben it looked to Stacey like he was nothing but a blur.

"Boss, welcome," the young man said in a New York accent, "I trust that you and your friend here had a safe and pleasant journey?"

Ben looked at him with a cold stare, "Lightspeed did you by any chance inform the mayor that I was coming today?"

Lightspeed looked at him and smiled, "Boss you know the mayor likes it when you visit this city."

He then paused for a moment as he turned his head at Stacey, winking at her he then turned around to face Ben.

"You know boss," he said as he was opening the door to the helicopter to fetch both their suitcases, "I informed the mayor only because I thought that it would be good publicity for you both."

Ben stood in the young man's way as he was making his way out of the passages seat.

"What does the mayor want?" He asked Lightspeed in an angry voice, "Only that you join him tonight for a charity gala boss."

Then Stacey came forward as she saw Ben's face getting red.

"Maybe Lightspeed's right, babe." She said in a soft voice, "Maybe this will increase our standing in this city and beyond."

Ben looked at her and then looked at Lightspeed, "OK Lightspeed. you have got Stacey's vote and mine now, inform Peter that we'll be coming tonight."

Lightspeed smiled as he took the cases and zoomed in with them to the penthouse. both of them followed slowly behind holding hands as they went in, as they both passed the doors Stacey found herself looking at a large reception area, like the one in Florida the floor was covered in marble only this was grey color, at the center of the room there was a large spiral staircase and towards the end was a fountain. Stacey turned her head towards Ben and smiled at him, he smiled back at her.

"Do you like it so far?" He asked her as Lightspeed came racing down from the stairs towards them.

"Cases are inside the master bedroom, boss," he said as he turned towards Stacey smiled at her.

Ben came towards the young man and put his hand over his shoulder

"Thank you Lightspeed for your help," he said smiling, "Why don't you go into the dining area and get Jack and yourself something to eat?"

The young man smiled at him as he raced towards one the doors at the right of the main entrance, Stacey looked at Ben in surprise.

"Is he really like that?" She asked him, Ben turned to her with a saddened look on his face.

"Lightspeed is the youngest mutant here, Stacey. Both of his parents were killed by a gang when he was just a small boy."

Stacey cover her mouth with one of her hands, "Babe, I didn't mean to judge."

Ben looked at her and faintly smiled, "it's OK Stacey, don't worry. I get angry with him but he's only trying to be helpful at the end of the day."

He then let go out her hand and started walking towards the spiral stairs.

"Come on Stacey," he said in a firm but polite voice, "I'll show you to our room."

Stacey grew excited as she heard him say that, "Please Ben, I can't wait."

hse then followed him slowly, it took them a few minutes to reach the top, like with the other penthouse there was a long corridor but unlike the other one the room wasn't the first on the left it was the first on the right next to the bathroom. Ben walked into the open door first and beckon her to follow, passing thought Stacey saw that is was simar to the layout of the other master bedroom in Florida, apart from the fact that this had no balcony. At the end of the room near a large window was a four poster bed, Stacey turned and smiled at Ben who had grabbed her hand,

"I think that I am going to enjoy my stay here with you Ben."

Ben gently hugged her and smiled, "I know that you are hun and I can't wait until tonight we are going to blow that gala out of the water."

CHAPTER TWENTY ONE

The Mayor's Gala

It was getting late in the evening as Peter Butler was waiting for one of his most important guests to turn up, he was a middle age man of average height with brown dark hair which now was greying, he was wearing a black suit with a red tie. Standing next to him was his wife, she was the same height has him she had long light brown hair and a kind face was far younger than her husband and ever since they had both been married people had questioned that she was only after his money, she was wearing a black colored evening dress with a pair of high heeled shoes. On both hands she was wearing a pair of long white opera gloves, she looked at her husband and smiled.

"Come on Peter," she said in a friendly but firm voice, "You can't stand out here all night waiting for our guests to turn up."

Peter turned toward his wife and smiled, "I know Rachel but I want to make a good impression with our guests especial our good friend Mr. Fox," Rachel smiled, "Is he coming then I thought that Ben was still serving in the military?"

Peter looked at his wife, "He's retired from the Military now Rachel, his main goal in life is to help kids to get off the streets and work towards a future."

Rachel smiled at Peter, "I know that he has helped you with you political career darling and you have helped him."

they both smiled at one another, as they were doing this a large black car pulled up outside the venue, Peter looked at it as a man in a black suit walked out. "Rachel, this looks like Ben."

The man in the black suit went over to the side door of the car and opened it, out of the car walked Ben he was wearing a blue colored suit and a black colored tie, as he climbed out of the car a woman came out with him. She was wearing a purple evening dress with a slit down the middle exposing her large cleavage, on her feet she wore a pair of purple high heeled shoes and on her hands, she was wearing a pair of long purple opera gloves. On her face, she was wearing purple eyeshadow and on her lips, she wore purple-colored lipstick, she looked normal to both Peter and his wife apart from the fact that she had light green colored skin. As soon as they were both out of the car Ben and the green-skinned woman began walking towards Peter, seeing him Peter smiled.

"Ben. welcome buddy." Ben took Peter by the hand smiled.

"Thank you for the invite, Peter," he said as he smiled and made his way over to Rachel, "Rachel you are looking as lovely as ever."

Rachel smiled at him, "You'rw the same charming young man as ever, Ben," she smiled, she then looked over at Stacey, "Who is this young woman Ben, your girlfriend?"

He then smiled at Rachel, Tthis is Stacey, my girlfriend." Stacey blushed as Ben smiled at her, he then turned towards her.

"Stacey, I like to introduce you to Peter and Rachel Butler the mayor and mayoress of New York City and old friends of mine." Peter took one of Stacey gloved hands and kiss it.

"It's a pleasure to meet you, Stacey." he said as he turned toward his wife smiling.

"Ben, why didn't you tell us that you had a girlfriend?" Rachel said as he was smiling along with her husband, Ben looked at them both Stacey could tell he was slightly embarrassed.

"Ben and I have only just got together." she said in a soft but firm voice.

Both Peter's and Rachel's faces dropped as they heard this, Ben then stood with Stacey not saying anything, after a few minutes he then broke the silence, "Can we go in?"

Rachel turned and smiled, "Of course Ben, all of the guests have turned up now so there is no point in standing outside any longer."

Ben smiled at her and took Stacey by her hand and followed them through two large glass door. As they were following the couple Stacey couldn't help but think about the way her life had gone since she had met Ben again, as they passed the main doors they came into a large corridor filled with pictures and photos, Stacey looked at one photo that showed Ben shaking hands with Peter. In this photo he looked younger and looking, she then rushed off as both she and Ben continued to follow, coming to the end of the corridor they then turned left and were lead into a large hall. Inside there was a large table with food and on the floor spread out was a long red carpet, both Stacey and Ben looked at each other and they saw the number of people that had been invited, at the far end of the hall was a large stage with two red colored curtains hanging down from both sides.

Peter then turned to them both smiling. "Ben, I'm just heading up to the bar do you and Stacey want to go with Rachel and get a table?"

Ben nodded in response as he took Stacey's hand again and followed Rachel, before he could do this he was stopped again by Peter.

"What would you both like to drink?" He asked smiling, Stacey looked at him and smiled back.

"I'll have a gin and tonic please."

Peter then looked at Ben, "Ben what are you having buddy?"

Ben gave him a friend smile. "That's very kind of you Peter, I'll just have a double whiskey please."

Peter smiled at them both and walked slowly off to the bar in the far side of the hall, as he was doing this both Stacey and Ben saw Rachel sitting at a table near the stage. They both walked up to it and sat next to her, Stacey sat down next to her whist Ben sat opposite.

"You two look lovely tonight." She said smiling at them both.

"Ben, please tell me how did you and Stacey meet?"

Ben looked at Stacey and then back at Rachel.

"We met in a medical center." he said.

"Not one of those centers that experimented on people?" Rachel asked in an angry voice.

Stacey looked at her puzzled, "Yes but, how do you know about those?"

Rachel gave her a friendly smiled. "Because my dear, I don't know if Ben has told you this, but me and my husband are mutants."

Stacey covered her mouth as if to be sick.

"Ben," she said in an angry voice, "Why didn't you tell me?"

He looked at her and then turned his head seeing Peter coming back to the table holding a tray of glasses, he then turned his head back around to Stacey.

"I didn't think that it would matter."

Hearing this Stacey walked out, leaving him, Peter and Rachel, Rachel looked at him and gave him a cold hard stare.

"I think that you better go after her Ben." She said in an angry tone, "You don't want to leave her alone now do you?"

CHAPTER TWENTY TWO

Ben's Revelation

Stacey could feel herself getting angry as she ran towards the main entrance of the hall, as she ran towards the large glass door that she looked behind her thinking that Ben was following her, she was in luck as he was not wear to be seen. As she pulled the door open there was a surprise waiting for her on the other side it was Ben, Stacey slowly walked towards him closing on of her gloved hands into a fist.

"You lied to me, Ben." she said as she drew nearer to him. She then stopped for a moment and looked at him puzzled.

"Hold on," she said as she dropped her hand, "How did you get out here so fast?"

"He had help," a female voice said coming form behind him, standing next to Ben was Rachel.

Stacey looked puzzled as she saw them both, Ben walked slowly up to his girlfriend.

"I can see that you are confused, Stacey please allow me to explain. Rachel had the ability to walk thought solid objects that why I came out of the hall so quickly."

Stacey walked slowly away from him as she saw Rachel walking up to them both,

"Stacey." Rachel shouted in a friendly voice, "Ben was only thinking of you and held your best interests at heart."

Stacey slowly turned her head towards the other woman and gave her an angry grin.

"Why is he so close to you and your husband?" She said as she began to grit her teeth.

Rachel turned and looked back at Ben and then back to at Stacey.

"Ww are close with him because he is like our family." Stacey stopped again for a moment and began listening, "You see Stacey, after your escape at that medical center, Ben and the other test subjects were branded as failed experiments."

Stacey looked at her impatiently, "What has this got to do with you and your husband?"

Rachel gave her a cold look, "I'm just getting to that."

Ben looked up at her and smiled faintly, "Now, my future husband Peter who wasn't the mayor at that time worked as a lab assistant for Dr. Young, this was all just a cover as he stole some of that serum to test it out on himself."

Stacey eyes widen as she heard this.

"So he was a spy then?" She asked surprised, Rachel nodded and smiled faintly.

"And where were you in all of this?" She asked as she could feel herself getting angry again.

"I was being held in a lab with Ben," she said as she paused for a moment, "As we were being held Peter began injecting himself with the serum in the next room to us. After a few minutes there was a loud bang followed by a load of people screaming."

Stacey looked at both her and Ben.

"I still cannot understand why you didn't tell me Ben." She said crying, Ben slowly came up to her and put his arm around her waist.

"Stacey, that night I thought that I was going to die and if it hadn't been for Peter then you and I wouldn't be standing here." He then paused and looked over at Rachel and then back at Stacey, "If Peter hadn't provided us with the distraction that we needed then we would have never have gotten out of that place alive."

Stacey then looked at him and smiled.

"But we are alive aren't we?" She said smiling, "what happened after you escaped?"

Ben's head dropped and he began to clenched his hands into fists, "After my escape, I tried to find my family but the military beat me to it."

He then paused and took a deep breath, Stacey looked at him in shock. "What happened, Ben?"

He then turned away from her and looked at Rachel/

"Stacey, Ben's family like mine and the rest of the subjects had been placed under arrest and taken to a secret facility," Rachel had her head lowered, "We never got to see them again."

Stacey then slowly went up to Ben and put on of her hands on his shoulders.

"Ben I'm sorry," she said as she put her arms around him, as she did this she looked at Rachel. "How did you and him meet up again?"

Rachel gave her a faint smile. "Ben had decided to go away for a few weeks to Florida, when he got there he met me again only this time I wasn't on my owe Peter was with me."

Ben then looked at Stacey and smiled, "At that time I was finding it difficult to control my powers, Peter helped me and encouraged me to help other mutants in return all he asked of me was to expand his political career so that he could hold influence in government on the treatment of mutants."

Stacey smiled faintly at her boyfriend, "So, Peter became a mentor to you then babe?" She asked as she saw him lighting up a cigar.

"Yes Stacey, but he became more than just a mentor, he became like a father," he then paused as he began to take a drag, "Peter was the one who encouraged me to set up the Haven program he also encouraged me to travel the world to look for mutants who would join our cause."

Stacey came over to him and put one of her gloved hands on his shoulder, "I think by right you have made him proud babe. as I'm proud of you."

As he heard this Ben let the cigar in his hand fall to the ground, he then grabbed Stacey and they started to kiss each other passionately, Rachel smiled as she watched them, she then passed thought the wall back to the party leaving them both alone.

CHAPTER TWENTY THREE

Greena

It was early in the morning as Trisha was getting out of bed, as she got up she viewed her surroundings, she was in a square-shaped room that was near to Dr. Young's lab. At the far end of the room in the top right hand corner was a small window slit, Trisha could see the sun's first rays coming thought as she threw off the green colored sheet that had been covering her, she then threw herself from the top bunk bed that she had been sleeping on and onto the ground. As she landed she bent his knees slightly and jumped away from the bed, she then lay onto her chest and starting doing some press ups, once she had done ten she rose back to her full height and smiled to herself. She then went back over to the bottom bunk to get changed as she was wearing only a brown colored bra and underwear, as she was getting changed she heard a knock coming from the door.

"Come in, the door's open," she politely said as she put a black colored t-shirt on and a pair of grey trousers.

As the door opened Dr. Young walked into the room, she was wearing a lab coat and had a surgeons mask on her face, on both of her hands she wore a pair of latex gloves, Trisha looked at her and stood up in surprise saluting her.

"Dr. Young," she said in a surprised voice, "I didn't realize that you were coming."

She stopped for a moment as the doctor came forward.

"I have good news Trisha," she said in a friend and confident voice. "The test's that I carried out on you proved positive,"

Trisha looked at her eyes wide in amazement, "So does that mean that I can be part of your super soldier program then, Doctor?"

Dr. Young nodded and smiled, "Out of all the volunteers who came before you, you are the most physicallu fit."

Trisha smiled, "Thank you Doctor,. but could you please tell me what effect will the serum have on me and my body?"

Dr. Young smiled as she came closer to the young woman, "I'm very glad that you have asked me that question," she said in an almost playful voice as she sat next to her on the bunk bed, "The serum will increase your strength, speed, and stamina."

Trisha turned to face her, she then started to smile, "Really. so I'll be super strong then?"

Dr. Young smiled back at her, "Not only that but you will have super healing abilities and also you will be super attractive."

Trisha looked at Dr. Young face and smiled again at her, "Cool, I can't wait for you to inject me. When can you start?"

Dr. Young slowly sat up and turned to face Trisha, she then held out one of her hands, "We can start now if you like Trisha."

Trisha not thinking about anything else grabbed her hand and was pulled up from the bed, Dr. Young then lead her out of her room and into a corridor, she then turned right and passed through a door into her lab. Inside there were thousands of test tubes, organs from different types animal, all different types of plants and in the middle of the room, there was a bed. As she walked in Trisha looked at the specimens in amazement.

"Wow, so you are a real scientist then after all."

Dr. Young smiled at her as she sat down on a desk, "Trisha. science has always been my life," she said as she went over to a desk and keeled down having her back turned.

Looking at her it seemed to Trisha that she was looking for something inside the desk but what? As Trisha was thinking she heard Dr. Young's voice.

"Found it at last," she said as she began to stand up.

In her left hand she held a glass vial containing an odd green colored liquid, Trisha looked at it as she began pouring it into a siring.

Once she had done this she came over to Trisha with it and lowered her mask so that she could see her face smiling.

"Is that the serum?" Trisha asked her in a soft voice/

"it is my dear," Dr. Young gently said as she covered her face again with the mask. She looked at Trisha and pointed with a finger to a chair in the far left corner of the lab.

"Would you mind, Trisha?" she asked in a soft voice, "Stripping off to your underwear and sitting down please?"

Trisha nodded as she slowly took the t-shirt off that she had been wearing, next came the trousers, Dr. Young slowly watched her as she undressed herself to her brown colored underwear and smiled as she sat down in the chair. As she was sat down Dr. Young slowly walked up to her the siring in her left hand, Trisha stared at her and then at the syringe.

"Keep still for me please Trisha, as this might hurt a bit."

Trisha looked away and began grinding her teeth as Dr. Young injected her in her arm using all of all the liquid in the siring, as she was withdrawing it Trisha could feel a burning sensation in her entire body, as she looked at her arms she noticed that her skin was starting to change color. She then noticed that it was not just her arms that were changing color but the rest of her body, for an instant she felt like the whole of her body was on fire as it started to stretch and warp, as this was happening Dr. Young watched with an evil smiled upon her face. Once her transformation was complete Trisha was now sat on the floor the chair that she had been sitting on was broken, she had now grown much taller than she had been before she had been injected with the serum and her hair was now long and thicker than it had been, her chest and arms were ribbed with muscles and her skin was now light green in color. As she was getting up Dr. Young walked up slowly to her and held out one of her hands/

"Well, how do you feel?" she asked in an impatient voice.

Trisha put one of her hands against her forehead. "I feel like I've got a massive headache from hell Doctor, but apart from that I'm fine."

"is that all?" Dr. Young snapped at her.

"Well, for some odd reason," Trisha said in a soft voice "It looks like my skin has changed color but that can't be right can it?"

Dr. Young then yanked the mask off from her face and smiled at her, Trisha looked at her with a puzzled look.

"What's so funny, Doctor?" She asked in a soft voice.

"You really are simple aren't you, Trisha?" She said in a mocking tone as she walked over to her desk.

On the side there was a small hand mirror, she picked it up and walked over to Trisha, she place it into one of her hands and Trisha began to look at herself. She then let out a scream and then dropped the mirror which broke into pieces as it hit the floor.

"What have you done to me?" She said as she stood up and began to run towards the doctor with both of her hands out ready to grab her by her neck, Dr. Young remained calm as she just stood at her desk.

"I thought that you wanted to become part of my super soldier squad." She said as Trisha grabbed her by her neck.

"I did," she said as she began to tighten her grip, "But I didn't want to end up like a freak,"

Dr. Young smiled as she heard her say this, "Is this now how you see yourself Trisha, a freak?"

Trisha loosen her grip, "What is that suppose to mean?" She asked in an angry voice.

Dr. young smiled at her, "I see that you have been given a gift Trisha, a gift that can be used for the greater good."

Trisha gave her an angry stare, "Well whatever this gift is I don't want it make me normal again now!"

Dr. Young gave her a surprised look, "I can't, not yet anyway."

Trisha tighten her grip around Dr. Young's neck, "Why not, are you afraid that you might lose a potential super weapon?"

Dr. Young's face dropped as she heard this, "Let me go and I'll tell you then."

Trisha then loosen her grip around her neck and then let her drop to the floor, Dr. Young then picked herself up and walked slowly up to her desk. She then pulled open a drawer and pulled a photo out, she then walked slowly back to where Trisha stood.

"Are you aware of a young woman by the name of Stacey Roberts?" She asked.

Trisha eyed her slowly, "I don't know anyone by that name Doctor." she said in an angry voice, "What does that name have to do with me?"

Dr. Young again smiled, "Everything Trisha. You see Stacey was once a test subject but she escaped, I need your help to track her and her boyfriend down."

Trisha's eyes widen as she heard this, "And what do I get out of this for helping you?" She asked again in another angry tone.

Dr. Young smiled faintly at her, "I'll provide you with a serum that will turn you back into a human again." she then put her hand to Trisha to shake, "Will you help me Trisha, do we have a deal?" Trisha then looked at her, "I guess I don't have much of a choice, do I?"

She then reached for the doctors hand and began shaking it.

"By the way Doctor." she said "Don't call me Trisha anymore, call me Greena."

Dr Young smiled, "Very well, Greena." she said as she began laughing to herself.

CHAPTER TWENTY FOUR

The Visit from Mist

It was earlier afternoon as Stacey was in the penthouse's drawing room, she was sat back on a brown leather sofa with both of her eyes closed, she was wearing a black top and a short denim skirt her long blonde hair was now in a pony tail. As she was relaxing she heard footsteps coming towards her, they stopped as they neared the sofa, Stacey could feel a pair of hands touching her waist she then opened her eyes slowly. As she did this she saw Ben smiling at her.

"You took your time, Ben," she said as he parked himself next to her.

"Sorry hun," he said as he put one of his arms behind her and started to gently rub her back, "Was I gone long?" He asked as she moved closer to him.

Stacey smiled back at him as she rested her head against his chest, "You took your time, where were you?"

He smiled as he pulled something out from one of his jacket pockets, it was a small blue velvet box, holding it out in his hand he held it out showing it to Stacey.

"What is it?" She asked him in a soft voice, Ben smiled at her.

"Why don't you open it?" He asked, Stacey took it from his hands and slowly began to open the small box, inside she was surprised at what she found.

Inside the box being held in place was a white gold ring with a large cut diamond in the center, Stacey took it out and held it up smiling as she did. "It's beautiful Ben, but how much did this cost you?"

Ben then grabbed both of her green hands and looked at her smiling as he did. "It was $5600 for that ring Stacey,"

Stacey looked at the ring and then at him, "$5600?! Babe, are you sure that you can afford that?"

Ben smiled at her as he put one of his hands around her back.

"Stacey," he said in a soft voice, "I want you to know that I care about you because I love you, money will never be an issue for me as I have enough of it."

Stacey looked at him as she grabbed him around his waist, she then started rubbing his chest with one of her hands, Ben fell back in the chair as he closed his eyes. He then felt her warm smooth green skin on one of his legs, she rested her head on top of his chest, Ben then opened his eyes and looked down at her. She then looked up at him and smiled. "I love you Ben Fox more than anything else in this world."

Ben smiled at her and gently kissed the top of her head, "I love you also. Stacey more than ever."

They then looked at each other as they sat up, with out warning Stacey grabbed hold of Ben's face and started kissing him, as she kissed him Stacey started to unbutton his shirt exposing his chest, for a moment she stopped looked at him and smiled. Then she slowly took off the black top that she was wearing exposing the blue colored bra that she was wearing underneath, seeing her do this Ben slowly took off the pair of trousers that he had been wearing exposing a pair of white colored boxer shorts, Stacey smiled as she saw him in them.

"Sexy," she said as she started to laugh, she then slowly started to undo her skirt, she then slowly let it drop to the floor.

Ben looked at her as she lay herself over him, he felt her warm smooth naked green skin next to his, they then were going to kiss each other, as they were about to do this this he stopped raising his head. Stacey looked at him puzzled. "What's wrong, babe?"

Ben looked at her with a worried look on his face, "Stacey, I sense someone in this room with us."

Stacey gave him a puzzled look. "That's crazy," she said in an angry voice, "You know the same as I do that Lightspeed is out with chef in the dining area and you know he doesn't like coming in here."

Before she could say anything else there was a wisp of blue colored smoke coming into the room, it settled near the sofa and stopped, both of them got up and saw the smoke forming into a woman. It was Mist and from the look on her face Ben could tell that she was worried about something.

As she saw him she slowly walked over to him, "Ben, I need to talk to you, it's important,"

Stacey gave her an angry look, "Mist, both me and Ben are in the middle of something, can this wait?"

Mist gave her an angry look back, Ben looked at her as he stood up, "What's this about Mist?"

Mist then sat down on the sofa beside Stacey, "Yesterday we had a new member joining us at Haven Ben someone, calling herself Trisha Morgan."

Ben looked at the other woman puzzled, "Yes. so we get new members joining us all the time, what's so important about this one?"

Mist's face dropped and Ben could tell that she was worried about something.

"Ben," she said in a low voice, "This girl looked very much the same as her here."

Ben looked at her and didn't say anything, "You mean another me?" Stacey sharply interrupted.

Mist looked at her and gave her a nod, "Yes. it looked like that she has your green skin color, the dark green eyes, lips and nails but there is something different about this woman."

Ben again looked at Mist, "What is different about this one Mist?"

Mist looked at him her expression on her face remained the same, "She has long red colored hair and looks stronger, stronger than even her,"

Stacey turned back to him and grabbed his hand. Ben looked over at her and then back at Mist.

"Do you think that it's the military again planning another attack?" She said as she saw him getting up.

Ben turned towards Stacey and then back at Mist, "I don't know but this gives me idea, where is this woman now?"

Mist stood up and went over to him, "She's in the basement in a cell I ordered Powerhouse to keep her there until you returned."

Ben turned towards the sofa and then raised his hands his shirt and trousers levitated and fell into his hands.

"Good," he said as Mist smiled, he then turned to her and smiled back, "Go back to Haven and await my return there I will meet this other girl and read her mind."

Mist then nodded and in a flash she disappeared, He then turned back to the sofa and towards Stacey who was still lying down.

"Stay here Stacey," he said in a commanding voice.

Stacey looked at him with an angry look on her face, "Why do I have to stay here? Can't I come with you?"

Ben looked at her, "it's too dangerous now more that ever, especially if this new girl is stronger that you."

Stacey gave him another angry look, "I took Jenifer down didn't I?"

Ben gave her a sad look, "Stacey she was acting out of anger and rage, you beat her only because of one thing and one thing along that serum that she used on her was only a test sample nothing more."

Stacey's mouth dropped open, "You mean that she was only being used as a dummy?"

Ben nodded in agreement, she then stood herself up and moved towards him throwing her arms around him. "I still want to go with you, please let me."

He then looked into her dark green eyes and smiled.

"Stacey," he said in a low voice, "You can come, but please don't follow me to the basement. I want to deal with this woman myself."

Stacey nodded in agreement and threw herself back onto the sofa with him.

CHAPTER TWENTY FIVE

Ben's vision

It was getting late at night as Stacey and Ben made their way back to Florida, he had wanted to leave Stacey at his New York penthouse for her own safety, this had nearly caused Stacey to break down as she loved him and didn't want him to leave her behind. Ben and her then had taken a private jet back home as this was the quickest mode of transport, as Ben sat in a seat next to the window Stacey sat next to him, she was wearing a black leather bra and a pair of tight leather shorts and on her feet she wore a pair high heeled ankle boots. Ben was wearing a grey colored shirt and a light jacket, he wore a pair of green light trousers and a pair of sandy colored desert boots, Stacey looked at him as they both sat down and grabbed his hand. Ben looked at her and could tell that she was worried.

"Babe," she said in a soft low voice, "What do you think that we will find from this woman when you read her mind?"

He then looked at her and lowered his head.

"I don't really know Stacey," he said in a low voice, "Maybe I'll find who she is working for or what she wants who knows?"

Stacey looked at him and gave him a faint smile.

"I know one thing Ben," she said in a soft voice.

He looked at her and smiled back, "And what's that Stacey?"

Stacey gave him a grin showing him a set of perfect white teeth, "I love you and I always will love you forever,"

She then gave him a kiss on his cheek and sat back on her chair closing her eyes. Ben did the same but before he did anything else he took Stacey's hand and held it, it was earlier morning as the plane landed at the airport and he was the first to get up, as he was sitting up he turned to Stacey who was now asleep,

"Stacey." Ben said as he gently nudged her, "Stacey. it's time to get up, the planes landed."

Stacey's eyes flicked open and stared straight at into his eyes. She looked at him and smiled, "What time is it babe and where are we?"

He smiled faintly back at her, "it's five o clock in the morning babe. and we have arrived at Florida airport."

Stacey looked at him in surprise, "What we arrived here quickly then didn't we? Are we getting a lift back to Haven from here?"

Ben smiled again at her, "Powerhouse is picking us up from terminal 1."

Stacey didn't say anything as both of them stood up from their seats, Stacey held out one of her hands to Ben he grabbed it and they both made their way off the plane and onto the runway. As they made their way down the plane's steps Ben let go of Stacey's hand for a moment, she turned and looked at him as he did this.

"Are you okay babe?" She asked in a worried voice.

He then started rubbing his head as if it was hurting him.

"I just had a premonition a vision into the future," he said as he took her hand again.

"What did you see?" She asked him as they both made their way off the stairs.

Ben stared at her and from the look he gave her Stacey could tell that he was worried, "I saw us both standing over the bodies of dead mutants and humans there was smoke and fire around us as if we were standing near the edge of a battlefield."

Stacey's mouth dropped as she heard this, "You mean like a war don't you, darling?"

Ben nodded, "A war between humans and the beast's that they created, there is more than what I saw in my vision but I'll tell you more when we get home," he said as they both passed into the main building.

As they passed through to the main door Ben could feel Powerhouse's present, they both passing into an open hallway and waiting for them at the end near an open door was Powerhouse, he was wearing a long black leather coat and a pair of black fingerless gloves. On his face he was wearing a pair of black sunglasses, when he saw them both he slowly made his way up to them, Ben could tell just by looking at the big mans face that he wasn't happy.

"Welcome home boss." he said was close enough so that he extended his hand to Ben, he then turned towards Stacey, "And to you Miss Roberts I trust that your trip was enjoyable?"

Ben looked at him and gave him a faint smile, "It was, thank you Powerhouse,"

The big man then turned his gaze towards the door and then at Ben again, "Are you ready to go back to Haven boss?"

Ben put his hand on one of the big man's shoulders and smiled, "Yes, we both are. Lead the way please."

Powerhouse then turned and walked slowly toward the door letting both him and Stacey following closely behind.

CHAPTER TWENTY SIX

An unexpected Alliance

The sun was rising in the sky as the car that Powerhouse was driving made its way back to the penthouse, sat in the back seats were Ben and Stacey both holding hands. Ben turned his gaze towards Powerhouse.

"What's the news with that new girl that you captured?" He asked as the big man held his gaze on the road.

"Don't know the full story, boss." he said as he turned the car sharply towards the left and went down a narrow lane, "All I know is that she wanted to speak with you."

Ben turned towards Stacey and then turned back towards the car's main mirror, "Speak with me for what?" He asked in a sharp voice.

"Don't know sir." the big man said as he continued to drive, "But I bet that it has got something to do with that attack."

He then turned back towards Stacey, "Are you alright darling?" He asked her in a calm and caring voice.

Stacey nodded her head saying nothing ever since Ben had told her about the vision that he had, all she could think about was what it could mean for them both? After ten minutes of being on the road, they finial arrived at the penthouse, standing guard at the main entrance was a small band of Ben's own private security forces, they wore a set of protective bulletproof black armor across their chests. On their heads they wore a helmet that covered their entire face leaving only their mouth's exposed, they were armed with small handguns,

Uzi and AK47's. As the car pulled into the penthouse's drive one of the guards came up to the window.

"Powerhouse." the man said as he lowered the window down, Powerhouse looked at the man.

"What's wrong, Johnson?" The big man growled making Johnson back away.

"Is Mr. Fox available?" He said in a worried voice, Powerhouse turned away from the guard and looked at Ben.

"Boss, you are wanted." he said as Ben let himself out of the car.

Once Johnson saw Ben getting out he ran over towards him, Ben looked at him as he fell on his knees.

"What's wrong? Is the situation under control?"

He asked as Johnson picked himself up, he stared into Ben's eyes and looked like he was about to cry.

"I'm sorry sir," the man said as his body started shaking with fear, "But it looks like that prisoner escaped,"

Ben's face grew red with anger, "Escaped?! How?! And when?!"

Johnson backed away, "I don't know sir, but it looks like that she hasn't been gone long."

Ben turned to Powerhouse who was now getting out of the car, he then turned back to Johnson. "Put the penthouse on high alert, I want that woman found and unharmed, do I make myself clear captain?"

Johnson stood up and gave a salute, "Yes sir. I'll tell my men to do a full sweep of the penthouse and the surrounding area, we won't let that woman escape."

He then made his way towards the entrance of the penthouse and too a small unit of security forces, Powerhouse then came up to Ben and rested a large hand onto his shoulder.

"Don't worry Boss, we'll get that woman." Ben turned his head and smiled at the big man.

"I know we will, Powerhouse," Ben then turned towards the car and saw Stacey getting out, rushing over he took her hand.

Stacey looked at him giving him a worried look on her face.

"Babe, what happened?" She asked, Ben, looked at her and smiled faintly.

"That prisoner that Mist told us about has escaped, my security forces are looking for her now as we speak." As he was saying this both himself, Stacey and Powerhouse heard shouting coming from inside the main reception of the penthouse.

Quickly all of them rushed through the door followed by a squad of security guards, as they came inside Ben could hardly believe his eyes standing in the middle of the room surrounded by a pile of broken bodies was the prisoner. Like Mist has said she had light green colored skin, dark green colored lips, eyes and nails and red colored hair, she looked just like Stacey apart from one difference her chest arms and legs were ribbed with muscles. She wore what looked like a pair of ripped jeans and a ripped white colored tee shirt, her long red hair was blowing, Ben took a look at her and then turned to face both Powerhouse and Stacey. Stacey looked at him with a worried look on her face.

"Ben." she said to him, "I'm afraid."

He then smiled faintly at her, "Don't be Stacey, it will be okay, I'll try and sort this out."

He then turned his back and took a few steps toward the woman, as he did this the woman stared at him closely. "Looks like I got your attention then."

Ben looked at her as he came closer, "You did." he said stopping for a moment as he scanned her with his mind, "My name is Ben Fox, and you call yourself Greena, right?" Greena stared at him in surprise her mouth dropped open as she saw him coming forward, "Your real name is Trisha Morgan and you served in the army in Iraq didn't you?"

Greena looked at him as if he had just come from another planet, "How do you know all of these things about me?" She asked sharply.

Ben laugh softly, "I'm a psychic and like you, I'm a mutant." Ben looked at the pile of bodies near them and then looked up at Greena, "You didn't kill those guards, did you?" He asked in an angry tone.

Greena looked at him and laugh, "No, they're just stunned that's all," she then looked at him and clenched one of her hand into a fist. "My real target is you and that other freak," she said in an aggressive tone as she looked over at Stacey, she then ran towards Ben with her fist out ready to hit him.

Ben raised his hand before she could land a hit and held her in the air, Greena looked at him in surprise and horror. "How did you counteract my attack?"

Ben smiled at her, "I knew that you were planning to attack me before you have even a chance to move."

He then lowered his hand and let her fall to the ground, Greena then went up. She then looked at him again, "I will kill you for that!"

Ben came forward and held out his hand to her, "You won't kill me, because you have been ordered to take me back alive to your leader."

Greena glared at Ben, "How much of my mind did you read?" She asked in an angered voice.

Ben again smiled at her as he helped her up, "Enough to know that your leader gave you those orders promising you a cure for the serum that turned you into this."

Greena looked away upset, Ben put on of his hands on one of her shoulders, "I am sorry my dear but your leaders have lied to you."

Greena looked at him and put her hands up to her eyes and started crying, "I'm nothing now but a freak, an experiment gone horribly wrong."

Ben looked at her and could see that she was very much like Stacey very attractive. He then held one of his hands out to her.

"You are not a freak Trisha," he said smiling, "You have been given a gift, one that you can used against the army and take your revenge."

Greena then removed her hands from her face, "How can I take revenge?"

Ben smiled back at her, "Because I am willing to offer you a place here at Haven and by reading your mind I know which base the military is operating from,"

Greena come forward to him and wiped her eyes.

"I'll gladly accept your help then, Mr. Fox." She said as she took his hand and started shaken it.

Stacey grew jealous as she watched as both of them smiled at each other.

CHAPTER TWENTY SEVEN

Stacey Jealous

Stacey was pacing up and down the corridor outside the office where Greena and Ben were talking, she had an angry look on her face as she was watching them both, Ben was standing up near his desk whilst Greena was sat down on a chair. As she was outside peering through the glass window at them both she heard footsteps coming from behind her, she turned around she saw Mist coming up the stairs to her, like Stacy she had a sour look on her face and she was angry. As she made her way up to landing she saw Stacey and stopped for a moment next to her, she then gently placed one of her hands onto one of Stacey's shoulders and looked at her.

"Hey there love, you okay?" Stacey looked surprised as she heard her ask her this.

"I'm fine, Mist" she said as she pulled away from her and turned back towards the window. Seeing her doing this Mist stood next to her, "Just look at them both." she said in an angry tone as she saw Greena laughing at something Ben had said, Mist again put one of her hands on one of Stacey's shoulders.

"Stacey," Mist said in a soft gentle voice, "I don't know about you but I do not trust this Greena."

Stacey turned towards the other woman and faintly smiled at her, it had been three days since Trisha had escaped from her cell since her escape she had been treated more like a guest than a prisoner and Ben had only made things worse by offering her a place in Haven. As she was smiling at Mist both of them heard the office door open, as it opened out walked Greena she was wearing a pink colored v neck top, on her waist, she was wearing a pair of blue jeans. As she walked out she turned her head towards the other two women and smiled, she then slowly made her way downstairs and vanished.

"What was that bitch smiling about?" Stacey asked as she turned her head back towards the window.

"More than likely Ben and her Stacey." Mist said in a sour tone, "she must have offered Ben something."

Stacey quickly turned around to face Mist clenching one of her hands into a fist.

"Like what Mist?" She said as Mist backed away from her.

"Stacey," Mist said in a worried voice "I don't think it is like that."

Stacey then lowered her hand and let it fall, "I'm sorry Mist I just don't what to do."

Before she could finish what she was about to say she heard the office door opening again, turning around both women saw Ben exiting. There was a faint smile on his face as he saw the two women, slowly he came up to them both and gently placed both hands on their shoulders.

"You seem happy Ben." Mist said to him in a soft tone.

Ben smiled at her and then turned his head toward Stacey, she looked at him and then turned away in disgust. Ben taking a back then looked at Mist with a puzzled look on his face.

"What's wrong with Stacey, Mist?" He asked in a puzzled tone.

Mist turned her hand towards Stacey and then quickly back toward him, she had an angry look on her face as she did this.

"Ben," she said in an angry tone, "Green Girl is angry because she and myself feel like you are spending too much time with that Greena."

Ben's face dropped as he heard this.

"What? You mean like a girlfriend don't you?" He asked surprised.

Stacey then came forward as she pushed passed Mist, "Don't try and lie to me, Ben Fox." She snapped, "I saw you in there with her and I know that you have got feelings for her."

As he heard this his face dropped in surprised.

"Look, you are getting the wrong idea, Stacey." He said as he walked towards her with one of his hands out.

As he was reaching out to touch her face with it she backed away from him,

"Don't lie to me, Ben! I want to know the truth about what you are really after with her." She said in an angry tone.

Ben then looked at her and lowered his head, "Ever since Trisha came here she has told me about that military base."

Mist came up to him and put one of her hands on his shoulders, "Is that true? Then you are not thinking about having an affair with her?"

Ben turned to face her.

"Why would you think that about me my dear Mist?" He asked in a soft but angry tone. Stacey came forward.

"We thought that you and her were involved and that you were going off me that's all." She said in a soft voice.

He then turned towards her and smiled, "That's not the case Stacey and you know it, I love you no one else." Stacey didn't say anything she lowered her head, Ben came forward and put his arms around her, "I just needed some information that she had that's all." He then kissed her head and then slowly turned towards Mist. "I want you to call a meeting please with all of our members."

Mist saluted him and smiled, "have you found out where the USA military is operating from Ben?" She asked, he smiled back at her.

"Yes I have Mist, from what our friend Greena told me, I have two names one Doctor Sarah Young and one LT John Watts."

Stacey let go of him for a moment as he turned towards her. "I'm sorry babe, did you say Doctor Young?"

Ben looked at her with a worried look on his face, "Yes Stacey, I did and I feel stupid that I didn't know this before,"

Mist then came forward. "The creator of the super soldier serum."

Ben turned to face her, "I m not surprised that she is involved in all of this, her and Watts must be working together." He then turned again to face Stacey, "Stacey I want you to go downstairs and gather everyone up to the office for a meeting, we are going to end the military plan." Stacey gave him a worried look.

"What if we fail?" She asked, Ben looked at her again and let out a deep breath.

"Then the military will be left unchallenged and unchecked, to top it off we'll be either become lab experiments or worse, dead."

Stacey nodded as he let go of her waist, she then followed Mist downstairs leaving Ben on the landing thinking about what to plan next.

CHAPTER TWENTY EIGHT

The Meeting

It was mid-afternoon as Stacey, Mist and the other members of haven gathered around a large black conference table in a small room next to the office, Stacey was sitting in between Mist and Powerhouse, sitting at the back end of the table wearing a blue suit was Frostbite. Stacey looked around and saw mutants that she had not seen before, next to Frostbite was a tall well-built man with flaming red colored hair and part of his face burnt, he wore a black colored jacket and trousers. Stacey eyed him for a moment then turned her gaze to another mutant that she hadn't seen before, she was was of average height with purple colored skin and medium dark green hair, she was sitting next to Greena. Stacey then turned to look at the chair at the end of the room and noticed it was empty.

"That must belong to Ben." She said to herself as she tries to relax.

As she was just getting herself settled the mutant who was sitting next to Frostbite got up from his chair and started ranting,

"Is this normal of Ben to keep us lot waiting like this or what?" As he was saying this all eyes turned towards him.

Frostbite who had been sitting next to him got up from his seat and gave the man an icy cold look, "He's busy Flamethrower and if I were you I would develop a bit of patience."

Hearing this Flamethrower sat back down in his seat.

"Please, accept my apologies Frostbite," he said in a more patience tone, "I'm just eager to fight these humans."

"You are eager Flamethrower," said the purple-skinned woman who was sitting next to him her tone was sharp, "Don't you think that we all are?"

As she said this Ben walked into the room as they saw him enter all of them stood up, Ben raised one of his hands gently as he guessed them to sit back down, as soon as they were seated Ben sat down next to Powerhouse.

"My friends," he said in a calm and clear voice, "Forgive me for being so late, there were a few things that I have to see to."

"What sort of things, boss?" Flamethrower asked him in an angry voice.

Ben gave him a hard stare. "I have been informed my dear Flamethrower by my dear friend Rachel Butler that my penthouse in New York has been attacked."

Hearing this Stacey went cold as she remembered Lightspeed.

"What has Peter done about this Ben? And is Lightspeed okay?" Frostbite said in a cold and icy tone.

Ben stood up and raised his hand to his old friend, "For the moment the boy, Peter and Rachel are safe." he then paused for a moment as he sat back down, "Peter is trying his best to overturn orders to give the army complete and total power to arrest any mutant's or anyone that they might suspect helping them." He then turned to Greena and then turned his head around to Stacey looking her in her eyes, "It's like I envisioned Stacey it's a total war."

"But we can win this, can't we Ben?" Asked the purple-skinned woman.

Ben turned to her and smiled faintly, "We can Violet, but we must act with caution."

Mist stood up and looked at him, "Are you seriously thinking of going after Dr. Young, Ben?" She asked in a worried voice.

"That would be crazy," said Powerhouse, "Some of us could die or worse, get captured."

Again Ben stood up and raised both of his hands, "What choice do we have?" He asked as he began to get angry, "We're dead if we stay here we anyway! If we take the fight to them we might win, so who's with me on this?"

Stacey stood up, "I'm with you babe."

Seeing this Greena stood up also.

"I'm also in on this," said Mist as she came forward.

Frostbite stood up and made his way over to Ben, "I know that you and I have always had disagreements in the past, but I'm with you on this also,"

Ben smiled at him, "You were always a hard one to please."

Frostbite started laughing as Flamethrower, Violet, and Powerhouse made their way up to Ben, Powerhouse smiled at Ben as he put one of his hands on the big man's shoulders, Violet put her arms around him and smiled and Flamethrower smiled also. Ben then turned and faced his small army as they began to line themselves up against a wall.

"This is it then everyone," he said in a low voice, "I will ask this only once anyone who does not want to throw their life away then please step outside now." As he was saying this no one moved, "Today we no longer are toys or tools of the government or the army we are free."

As he said this there was a loud cheer as all in the room threw their hands up and shouted together in a loud voice, "Down with the army! Down with the military!"

They then marched out of the office with Ben leading them onwards to victory.

CHAPTER TWENTY NINE

Ben's plan

It had been ten minutes since Ben had called the meeting, since then Stacey along with the other mutants had gone down to the armory in the penthouse's basement to get kitted up, as she entered the armory she made her way to a large locker. As she was opened it she looked to her right-hand side, as she did this she saw Mist, the other woman looked at her and smiled.

"Hey there Green Girl, look what I've got." She said as she held up two small handguns.

Stacey smiled back at her as she made her way over.

"Where did you get those guns, Mist?" She asked as she saw her friend looking at her and smiling.

"What, these things?" She said as she span them around before placing them back into the holsters at the side of her trousers, "I've had these guns for a good amount of time but I've never used them before, love." She said as she turned towards her locker and put one of her gloved hands inside.

Stacey didn't smile as she imaged herself fighting a war, "So it looks like that you are going to be using those guns and it also looks like that we are going to do some fighting doesn't it?" She said as she put one of her hands over one of Mist's shoulders, as she did this Mist turned around towards her and smiled.

"Stacey," she said in a soft but friendly voice, "We need to do this, otherwise what's the point of living?"

She then turned away from her and carried on, as she was doing this she and Stacey heard a loud noise coming from the end of the room, hearing this they both turned around in the direction of the sound and made they way towards it. As they both were making they way down towards the back end of the armory they both saw Greena, seeing them both she smiled and walked towards them.

"So, are you two ready?" She asked them as she started to laugh Stacey looked at her.

"Ready for what Greena?" She asked in a soft voice.

Greena came up to her and placed one of her hands on shoulders, as she did this Stacey could feel that like her skin was smooth. Greena and Stacey looked at each other something that they both haven't done before, as they did this Greena smiled at her.

"Ready to win this fight silly, have you forgotten already?"

Mist came forward and looked at her.

"Green Girl and myself are not the types to forget anything Greena."

She said as she raised her hand and started pointed a finger at her. Greena looked at her and smiled. "Relax will you? I was only joking with your friend here."

"Please don't make jokes about war." Shouted a male voice coming from behind both Stacey and Mist.

Both of them turned and saw Ben walking up towards them, he was wearing a long black overcoat with a pair of green colored trousers and a pair of black fingerless gloves, with him were Frostbite, Flamethrower, and Violet. As he approached them all three women stood up and saluted him, Ben looked at them,

"At ease, I don't want to make this like the army." he said as he smiled at Stacey.

Stacey smiled back at him as he made his way past her and slowly walked towards Greena, Once he had approached her he looked up at her.

"Are we both ready?" He asked her in a soft but firm voice.

"Ready for what, babe?" Stacey asked in a firm but fair voice.

Ben turned to her and smiled, "I've been thinking about things Stacey since our guest Greena arrived here." He paused for a moment as he took a deep breath, "Greena mentioned to me in my office about that base."

Stacey looked up at him as did the rest of the mutants.

"What about it Ben?" Mist asked impatiently.

He looked at her and giving her a faint smile. "What our friend here has told me Mist is that base is practical an impenetrable fortress impossible to attack directly."

Stacey came forward to him and touched his hand, Ben felt the warmth and smoothness of her green skin as she did this.

"What are you planning babe?" She asked him in a worried voice as she looked into his blue eyes.

Ben lets go of her hand and smiled at her, "My plan is Stacey, to get Greena to capture me and bring me before Watts and Young."

Stacey's face turned angry and she began to grind her teeth,

"Are you serious Ben?" She asked in an angry voice, "It's too rissky, you'll be killed or worse."

He then turned to her and let out another deep breath.

"Isn't this better than risking your lives on that base?" He asked her in an angry voice, "Besides, once I'm inside I'll escape."

Mist came up to him, "And then what Ben?" She asked in an angry voice.

Ben then looked her in the eye, "Then I'll be in contact with you all once I've lowered the bases security systems, then and only then will be our chance to attack."

He then looked around and saw that everyone in the room was nodding in approval all except Stacey who had her arms folded, he then came towards her and put a hand of her shoulder.

"Stacey." He said in a soft voice, "We have no hope of attacking that base directly it's best if I go." he then turned towards Greena, "Greena, are you ready?" He asked as the tall green skinned woman made her way towards him.

as she approached him she pulled a pair of handcuffs from out of her trousers pocket and snapped then around his wrists, he then walked with her towards the end of the basement and towards an open door. Before they both walked thought Stacey came running up behind them, Ben turned towards her and smiled faintly at her, she then looked at him giving him a worried look.

"Ben, I'm worried." she said to him as she put one of her hands on his cheeks.

"Don't be, everything will be fine." He said in a calm and relaxed voice.

"But what if you plan fails and you are killed?" She asked him her voice was soft and low,.

Ben looked at her with a calm look in his eyes, "Then I will name you as my successor of the Haven project. All of this will be yours."

He then turned and both he and Greena passed through the door leaving Stacey and the rest of the mutants to wait, Stacey didn't really know if she would see him again but what she did know was that he had complete faith in her.

CHAPTER THIRTY

The Temptation

It was early evening as a car went speeding down a highway, inside was Ben who was sitting in the passages seat and Greena who was driving, Ben who was now wearing nothing on his wrists looked at her. As he looked at her Greena turned the car sharply to the nearest exit and drove up, she then drove up to a near lay by underneath a bridge and stopped the car nearly sending Ben flying through the window. Ben looked at her and gave her an angry look as he pulled himself back on the car seat, as he did this Greena turned her head towards him.

"Why are you angry with me Ben?" She asked him in a soft voice.

Ben didn't say anything as he unfastened his seat belt and opened the car door before he could step outside he felt Greena's smooth green hand touching him.

"Are you alright?" She asked him in another soft caring voice.

He looked at her and took a deep breath, "I will be Greena, I'm just a bit afraid."

Greena looked at him with her dark green eyes Ben tried not to look as he was tempted to go and have an affair with her.

"Afraid of what honey?" She asked him in the same tone of voice that she had used with him before.

Ben then looked at her and from the look that he gave her Greena could tell that he was worried, "I had a vision, Greena. something terrible is about to happen but I don't know where or when it might happen."

Greena looked at him and gave him a reassuring look. "Ben, we're all afraid but you are the one who is keeping us strong, you have offered us hope."

He then faintly smiled at her, "I suppose that you're right Greena." he said as he got out of the car and lit a cigar, Greena looked at him carefully as he did this.

"You do realize that those things will kill you don't you?" She said in a caring but firm voice.

He then turned to face her and smiled ignoring her warnings.

"How far is that military base?" He asked as he puffed on the cigar.

Greena gave him a surprised look, "I'm warning you about your smoking habits and all you can do is to ask me about that base?"

Ben smiled again at her, "You worry too much Greena," he said as he walked towards the car holding the cigar in one of his hands.

"A mutants DNA is not like a human." He said as he sat sideways on the passages seat blowing out a perfect ring of smoke, "We can take a lot more than the average human-like for instance, we age a lot slower than they normally do."

Greena's eyes widen in surprise as he turned towards her and smiled.

"So Greena," he said as he throw the cigar onto the ground, "Where is this military base and is it far?"

Greena looked at him and smiled back showing him her teeth, "It's just passed this town and towards a beach."

Ben smiled at her again as he raised one of his hands up. Gently he held it up and placed it onto one of her cheeks, as he did this she began to close her eyes as if she was in a dream.

"Greena," she heard him say. "Thank you for doing this for me and my family."

Greena opened her eyes and looked at him, "Thank you for giving me a chance Ben."

Qithout warning she then closed in for a kiss, seeing this he backed away, Greena looked at him in surprise, "What's wrong honey, don't you like me?"

Ben looked at her and took a deep breath, Iit's not like I don't like you I really do, it's just I'm with."

"Green Girl?" Greena said sharply.

Ben nodded, "Look Greena I think that it's best if you and I remain friends also we should concentrate on this mission and not on our feelings."

Greena looked at him as he said this and from the look on her face he could tell that she was disappointed.

"What is it that you see in her anyway?" She asked him sharply.

Ben looked at her and then turned away, "She and I go way back. I met her in England when I was twenty-one."

Greena then put her hand on his cheek, "I heard that you and she were part of the first wave of test subjects is that true?"

He again looked at her, "Yes, it's true,"

Greena looked at him, "That is why you want to kill Dr. Young isn't it? Because she ruined both yours and Stacey's lives?"

Ben looked into her dark green eyes and could tell that she was playing with his feelings, "I wouldn't have said that she had ruined our lives as she changed them, what I would say is that she lied to us Greena."

Greena placed one of her hands on Ben's arms and brushed it slowly.

"You love Stacey, don't you?" She asked him in a very calm voice.

Ben looked at what she was doing and then looked up at her again, "Yes, I love her, and I would do anything I could to protect her, the same applies to all of the mutants under my protection."

He then looked at her and stared deep into her eyes, as he did this Greena started laughing, "So if I was a threat to Stacey and Haven, you would kill me then?"

Ben looked at her in surprise, "Why should you be a threat?"

He asked her in an angry voice, "No Ben I am not," she said calmly, "You opened my mind when you told me that Dr. Young had lied to me about there being a cure for that serum." She then turned to the steering wheel and started the cars engine, "However, I do have feelings for you and I am jealous of Stacey having you all to herself,"

Hearing this Ben banged the car door, he then looked at her, Iif you are jealous then Greena then I will have to do something that I will regret."

Greena turned and looked at him, "Like what honey?" She asked him in a curious voice.

"Like this." Ben said as he grabbed her and started kissing her full on.

As he did this Greena closed her eyes and put one of her hands down his trousers, Ben then put one of his hands over one of her large boobs, he knew full well that this was the only thing that would keep her from hurting Stacey, once they were both finished Greena turned towards him and smiled, she then licked the top of her dark green lip with her tongue and then turned toward the steering wheel. Once she had started up the cars engine she pressed her large foot on the gas pedal and the car raced away down the town towards the beach.

CHAPTER THIRTY ONE

Fooling Dr. Young

It was getting dark as Dr. Sarah Young was sitting at her desk in her lab, she had been typing a report all day and now she was about to shut her computer down before she had the chance to close the computer down the phone that she kept by her desk started ringing. Sarah who was now angry and tired slid her chair towards it and picked it up.

"Hello Young," she said in an angry voice.

"Hello Doctor," came a young woman voice.

"Greena?" Sarah spoke as she was surprised to hear her voice, "Is that you? Were you successful in completing your mission?"

Greena started to laugh as she heard her say these words. "You'll be very pleased to hear Doctor that I've captured Fox."

Sarah sat back at her desk chewing her lip and for a moment she said nothing as she held the phone in her hand away from her mouth.

"What?!" she finially said in disbelief as she held the phone up to her ear. "Are you being serious agent Greena?"

Greena paused for a moment and smiled, "If course I am Doctor." she said as she started laughing again.

Sarah smiled, "So, Ben's finial been captured then." She said as she began to laugh softly down the phone. "Greena," she continued, "Listen to me very carefully, I want you to bring him to my lab for examination."

Greena grinned as she heard this, "What about the rest of the mutants, Doctor? Don't you want me to round them up as well?" She asked in a wicked voice.

"No, not yet," Sarah said in a sharp and firm voice, "Just drop Fox off at my lab and then continue your hunt for the rest of them."

Greena laughed softly as held the phone, "No problem Doc, I'll have the rest of those freaks captured before the end of the day."

Sarah smiled again, "Just remember Greena, I want them alive and in good condition."

Saying this she put the phone down and sat back on her chair, meanwhile Greena who had parked the car by the base whilst she had been on the phone to Sarah turned to Ben, as she turned towards him he smiled at her.

"I must say Greena," he said in a friendly voice, "You put on a very good act there."

Greena smiled at him, "So, would you say that she fell for it then Ben?" She asked him as she placed a pair of handcuffs around his wrist's.

He smiled back at him, "I would say so, but we are going to have to be careful as she won't be fooled for long."

Greena threw back her long red hair as it fell towards one side of her face, "Ben once you get in that base how long do we need before we contact the others?"

He then pulled out a mobile phone with his free hand and gave it to her, "Take this." he said in a calm voice, "It has Frostbites number, once you contact him tell him to assemble the team."

She then nodded in response and then she gave him a puzzled look, "What about you, how long will you need?"

Ben looked at her and smiled. "Don't worry about me, I'll be fine," He then looked over towards the base and then back at Greena.

"Look, I'm ready when you are." He said to her calmly.

Before she got out of the car Greena lent over to him and gave him a quick peck on his cheek, she then smiled at him and then got out of the car, seeing this he followed her. As she closed both sets of doors his vision started to blur, as Greena turned she saw him falling to the ground. She then came running up to him with one of her hands out,

"Ben?" she asked as he picked himself up, "Are you alright?" She asked in a caring almost worried voice.

He looked at her and from the look that he gave her she could tell that he was worried.

"I had another vision," he said as he got back to his feet.

Greena looked at him and gave him a puzzled look. "What happened? What did you see?"

He gave her a faint smile but then fell again this time unconscious.

CHAPTER THIRTY TWO

Dr. Young's prisoner

It was daylight as Ben woke up after passing out, as he was coming too he viewed his surrounding, he found himself strapped to a bed inside what could only be Dr. Young's lab. As he was looking around he felt a sharp pain coming from his right arm, as he turned his head to look at his arm he grasped in horror, sticking out of his right arm injected directly into his vein was a large needle inside it was half filled with blood. Ben also noticed that he was half naked and that he had been linked up to a heart monitor, he then tried to struggle but found it useless as the straps held him firmly in place.

"Forget about escaping as your strapped down tight." He heard a familiar female voice saying.

Ben turned his head towards the left side of the room and as he did so he saw her.

"Dr. Young?" He said in a surprised voice.

Dr. Young smiled at him as she sat up from the chair that she had been sitting on and came over to the bed towards Ben.

"Hello Ben, did you miss me?" She asked as she started smiling evilly at him.

Ben gritted his teeth as he saw her, "I've been waiting for this." He said as he started to struggle.

"Why?" She asked him as she sat by the bed, "So that you can kill me for ruining your life?"

Ben didn't say anything back at first but as she said these words he could feel his blood boiling.

"You didn't just ruin my life but also the other so-called test subjects lives." He said in an angry voice.

hearing this Dr. Young snapped back, "I gave them a purpose Ben, like I did you and that girl that you are with now."

"Purpose?!" Ben answered back sharply, "What purpose?!"

Dr. Young looked at him as she put one of her hands on his face and gently rubbed it, "For the army of course, my dear Ben."

He looked at her and his face was full of anger and rage, "Yo be used as weapons of war, what you did was wrong and you know it."

As she heard this Sarah became angry herself and using her nails she slashed the young mans face leaving a large open cut,

"How can this be wrong, Ben?" She then asked him, "This could have saved lives in the field! Look at yourself, you have the ability to read minds, control people like puppets and on top of that you have the ability to look into the future." She then paused as she looked at him as she saw a trail of blood running down his face, "You and the rest of your gang are nothing but selfish," she said as stood up to her full height and towered over him, "But it doesn't matter anymore." She then went over to the main door but before she exited the lab she turned her head towards him and smiled, "You are now a prisoner here Ben, and what's even better you are going to help my research in a producing an even stronger solder serum." As she was saying this she turned her back and went through the door laughing as she went.

Ben laid on the bed angry and full of hate and rage, he then tried to calm himself down by closing his eyes and thinking of Stacey. As he was doing this he heard the lab door opening again, as it opened he became aware of another person in the room, he then opened his eyes and found that string him right in his face was his old friend Lt Watts. Watts looked at him and smiled.

"So Fox, finally decided to join the party huh?" He asked in a menacing tone.

Ben looked at him coldly, "Say that to me when I out of this bed Watts," as this Watts just laughed cruelly.

"I wouldn't think that yet if I were you, freak!" He said and his tone was mocking, Ben looked at him hard and coldly, "Command has issued an order on you'll little club." Watts continued as he made his way to the other side of the room away from the young man. "We are going to take all of you little friends by force." he said as he smiled at him, "Thanks to that friend of your girlfriend we now know where your base of operations is."

Ben gave him another cold stare and this time he spoke, "if you harm anyone in there Watts, I'll kill you."

Watts came up to him and grabbed him by his neck, "Is that a threat worm?" He said in an aggressive voice as he tightened his grip.

Ben looked at him and smiled, "Aren't I better to you and your girlfriend alive Watts?"

Watts lost his grip and looked at Ben in surprised, without warning he held both of his hands to his head and started screaming, at this Ben started smiling as he began to read his mind, as he was doing this he knew that Watts was lying about the attack but as he delved deeper he found something more. Dr. Young and the army were planning to capture mutants and using there genetic materials planed to clone them, as he found this from Watts Ben released him, as he was released Watts fell on both of his knees to the ground, he then looked up at him in anger and rage.

"Alright, that's it you little bastard." He said as he ran towards the bed with one of his fists out, "Time for me to knock some sense into your thick skull."

As he was about to strike the lab door opened again and in walked Greena, she looked at Ben and then she looked at Watts.

"Lieutenant, what are you doing to the prisoner?" She asked him as she walked into the room.

Watts looked at her with a face of rage, "I'm giving this no good son of a bitch a lesson in manners."

As he was about to hit Ben, Greena caught his hand, she then gave him a hard look.

"Didn't Dr. Young want no harm caused to him while he's here?"

Watts grunted at her and then pulled away, "You were lucky," He said turned to him before exited the lab. "When Sarah's finished with you it'll be round two for both of us."

He then exited allowing Greena to make her way up to the bed, as she did this she looked at his face.

"I'm sorry for allowing this to happen." she said as she grabbed a pack of wipes from the desk.

Ben looked at her as she wiped the blood from his face and smiled, "Don't be. Remember. I wanted to come here."

She then put one of her hands onto his chest, as she was doing this Ben looked at her and smiled faintly. "Did you manage to get in touch with Frostbite?"

As he said this she looked at him and returned the smile. "I did Ben and he said that he was going to call a meeting with the others."

He smiled at her again. Greena looked at him and lowered her head, "I've got to get you out of here Ben. I feel terrible about what's happened."

Ben looked at her and took a deep breath, "Please listen- if you can, Greena." he said in a worried voice, "Can you get in touch with Frostbite again?"

Greena nodded at him, "Yeah, sure I can honey. Why?"

He then looked at her again and she could tell that he was bothered about something,

"I scanned Watts mind and what I found surprised me." He said in a worried voice.

"What did you find honey?" Greena asked as she sat down on the bedside, Ben let out another deep breath.

"They are planning to use our genetic material to create copies," Greena gave him a puzzled look.

"You mean like clones?" He nodded his head as she stood up. "I'll contract Haven straight away honey you have my word on that."

Ben smiled at her as he lay back down.

"Just don't let anyone know that you are working with us now, Greena." He said as she ran out of the door.

He then put his head down and then tried to get a bit of sleep for he knew that it would not be too long before Frostbite, Stacey, and the rest of his mutants rescued him and this war would soon be over.

CHAPTER THIRTY THREE

The Rescue Mission

Stacey sat impatiently in a chair in the large conference room by the large table as she was waiting for Frostbite to call the meeting, as she was waiting she began to tap her long green nails on the table, as she was doing this she noticed Mist entering the room. Seeing her Stacey stood up from where she had been sitting and went over to her, Mist saw her and smiled faintly at her.

"Hey Mist." She said as she returned the smile back, "Have you heard anything from Ben and Greena?"

Mist shook her head, "Like you Green Girl, I haven't heard anything for either of them in two days.

"I wonder if they have both run into trouble?" Stacey asked in a puzzled voice as Mist looked at her.

"That could explain the reason why Frostbite has called this meeting," Mist said in a worried voice.

Stacey gave her an angry look, "I swear Mist, if that bitch Greena has betrayed Ben she'll answer to -."

As she was about to finish her sentence Frostbite walked in, with him was Violet, Powerhouse, Flamethrower, and Shifter, from the look on his face Stacey could tell that he had bad news, as he made his way to the end of the table he ordered his followers to sit down. Seeing the rest of the mutant's sitting both Stacey and Mist sat down, Frostbite then spoke as soon as everyone has taken their place.

"Everyone please listen up." He said in a worried and frightened voice, "I regret to say this but Ben has been captured by Dr. Young and her allies."

"Captured?! What do you mean captured?" Asked Violet her voice was cold and unforgiving.

Powerhouse turned and face her, "It's that green-skinned bitch she's betrayed him hasn't she?"

As he heard this Frostbite slammed his hand down on the table. "That's enough of that, Powerhouse! Greena's on our side and the boss trusts her like he trusts us."

"So how's the boss managed to get himself captured them Frosty?" Asked Shifter in a puzzled voice, "I mean it's not like him to go down without a fight."

Frostbite turned towards him, "I don't know Shamus, but what I do know is that at the moment, he is in a lab there being tested on."

"Tested on?! You mean like some sort of twisted experiment?" Stacey asked in a frightened voice.

Frostbite stood up from his chair and went over towards her.

"Stacey," he said in a cold but far voice, "I don't know what is happening at that base but according to Greena, Dr. Young and the army want to get their hands on our DNA and the boss is their first test subject."

Mist who had been sitting next to Stacey stood up from her chair, "So Frostbite how are we going to break him out?"

Violet who was sitting a few yards from her shouted over, "Can't you teleport us all to that base Mist? We could launch our attack."

Powerhouse interrupted. "Didn't you hear Violet?" He said in an angry voice, "That base is an impenetrable fortress as soon as we go inside we'll be picked off one by one."

Mist looked at him and lowered her head, "So what do we do now then, just wait?"

Shifter then slammed his hand onto the table, "No we can't wait," he said in an angry voice. "We all owe the boss that honor if it was one of us what do you think he would do?"

Frostbite turned and eyed him, "Do you have a plan Shamus or are you just wasting time?"

Shamus smiled at the taller man, "Yes I do have a plan what if Mist teleports only two of us?"

All of the mutant's in the room turned toward him and listened carefully to what the little man had to say/ "Yes. What if we only send two mutant's out? That way we could do two things at once, rescue the boss and shut that damn security system down."

Frostbite smiled, "That sounds like an excellent plan Shamus but who should we send?"

"I'll go!" shouted Stacey, as she said this all of the other mutants in the room looked at her their eyes widen in surprise.

"Why are you volunteering yourself to go Stacey? So only get yourself killed?" Violet asked in an angry and cold voice.

"I volunteer myself because unlike the rest of you I can use stealth and the element of surprise," she said back in a more angry voice, "And I think that Shifter should come too as he will be able to disguise himself as one of the soldiers in that base."

Shifter smiled as he heard this, "I really like this girl. See Frosty I told you that I have got quite the following didn't I?"

Frostbite didn't say anything as he made his way back to the end of the table, as he sat back down he looked at Stacey and smiled, "Stacey once you and Shifter are in that base I want you to contact me, is that clear?"

Stacey looked at him and smiled back, "Understood Frostbite." sSe said in a confident voice.

Frostbite then turned to Mist, "Once you have teleported Stacey and Shifter into the base teleport yourself back here."

Mist didn't say anything she just saluted him, again Frostbite looked over at Stacey, "I am counting on you Stacey and you too Shifter once that security system is down then we can make our way into that base and being our attack." He then paused as he saw Stacey, Mist and Shifter standing in a circle holding hands, Hgood luck to you both. Be sure to keep in contact with me once you have Ben and once that system is down."

Stacey smiled at him, "Son't worry Frostbite, we'll get it done won't we Shamus?"

"Oh yes, lass," Shifter said, before he or Stacey could say anything else all three of them disappeared in a puff of blue smoke.

Frostbite smiled, "Godspeed to you all." He shouted as he went back to his chair and sat back down.

CHAPTER THIRTY FOUR

Ben's Puppet

Ben was restless as he tried to get to sleep it had been well over two hours since Greena had seen him, as he closed his eyes and rested his head on the pillow underneath him he felt someone else who was now present in the lab, opening his eye he spotted a young female lab assistant by Dr. Young's desk. She had long dark brown colored hair and was slim built, for some reason she had her back turned to him, Ben smiled as an idea came into his mind what if he could escape using her as his puppet? He closed his eye and began to concentrate, at first the young woman didn't seem to notice anything as she came up to him, looking at him she gently pulled the needle from his vein in his arm taking the needle and putting it inside one of her lab coats pockets. As she was covering his arm with a cotton wool bud and a piece of micropore tape she felt a sharp pain coming from inside her head, she stopped for a moment as she raised both of her hands to her head and screamed in pain. In an instant it was over as Ben had complete control over her mind, he then opened his eyes and found her standing in front of him her face reminded him of Stacey's as she led over to him.

"Get these restraints off me." He said in a commanding voice as the woman went over to the desk.

By the desk there was a small computer console with a large row of buttons in the middle there was a large red button, as the young lab assistant pressed it the restrains that had kept him strapped to the bed fell away, Ben got up to his feet and slowly went over to desk and over to the computer as he was logging on he became aware of three more mutants somewhere in the base. As he was logging on to the computer the woman stood over him and watched him, he turned his head towards her.

"Wait outside," he said to her in another commanding voice.

The woman turned slowly and walked out of the door and into the corridor, as she Ben turned towards the computer which now was logged onto the user's screen, he looked at it and smiled as he clicked on Dr. Young's user's profile. As he did this it came up with a password protection screen, Ben smiled to himself since he had read John Watts mind he had laid everything bare to him about the base, computer passwords, security clearance even certain rooms in the base. Concentrating with the task at hand he then began entering Dr. Young's password, carefully he pressed the enter key and was pleased to find that the computer granted him access, as the desktop came up Ben clicked on the start menu bar. He then strolled over to the documents folder and clicked on it, as it opened the folder he noticed a document that had the name of serum, interested he pointed the mouse over it and began to open the document. Once the document had been opened Ben started to read it and found that not only did it contain the serum's ingredients but also it effects, Ben then pulled his hand into one of his trousers pockets and pulled out a USB drive, he then gently inserted it into the computer and made a copy of the document that he had been reading. Once he had done this he deleted Dr. Young's copy and shut the computer down, he then made his way out of the lab and to the assistant who had been standing waiting for him.

"Come on, let's go." he shouted to the woman.

As there were about to walk off from the lab he looked in front of where they were standing and spotted two figures coming towards them, both of these figures were slowly coming to towards them and from the look of them they were armed with weapons, Ben stood still with fear as his control over the lab assistant had drained his power level he closed his eyes waiting to expect the end. Without warning he heard footsteps coming from behind the two soldiers, he then could sense two mutants approaching, as they made their way behind the soldiers there was an unexpected silence as both men were knocked to the floor. he then quickly opened his eye to find both of the solder lying still on the ground, standing near them were Stacey and Shift, seeing her Ben came running towards her and fell into her arms.

CHAPTER THIRTY FIVE

Shutdown

Ben couldn't believe his luck as he held Stacey in his arms, as they both were hugging each other he then noticed that she was shaking.

"Stacey, is everything alright?" He asked as he let go of her.

tacey lowered her head and he could see tears streaming from her dark green eyes, gently he put on of his hand onto her cheek and started rubbing it.

Stacey looked up at him, "Ben I thought that I lost you."

He gave her a faint smile, "Lost me? What do you mean?"

Shifter came forward to him and put one of his hands on his shoulders, "What the lass means boss is, we thought that you had been killed."

Ben looked at the small Irish man and smiled, "Shamus, Stacey." He said as he smiled faintly at them both, "Dr. Young wanted me alive for her experiments."

Stacey looked at him her head was still down.

"What about Greena, Ben?" She asked him in a soft but firm voice, "Sid she betray you?"

He then looked at Stacey as he gently raised her head up, "Stacey, without her I would have never gotten into this base."

Stacey smiled at him showing him her teeth, "You really trust her don't you babe?"

She asked smiling as she did, Ben looked at her and smiled back, "I do, but not as much as you." Stacey smiled and then she turned towards the lab door and saw the lab assistant, "Who's your friend babe?"

She asked him in a soft voice, Ben turned his head round towards her and then back around to Stacey.

"Oh yeah, I almost forgotten about her," he said smiling, "I think that this is one of Young's assistants."

He then raised one of his hands and snapped his fingers, as he did this the assistant passed out against the door, Shifter ran towards her and both him and Stacey looked at him.

"Is she dead?" Stacey asked as she looked at him.

Ben gave her a faint smile, "No." he said as he slowly walked up to her and put his hand into one of her lab coats pockets, "Just out cold." He said as he turned towards Stacey.

Stacey looked at him puzzled as she noticed that in his left hand he was holding what looked like a glass vial, inside was a thick red colored liquid.

"Is that what I think it is boss?" Shifter asked as he saw Ben putting it inside one of his trouser pockets.

He turned and looked at Shifter and took a deep breath. "Yes Shifter, that is my blood inside that container."

Stacey came up to him and put one of her hands on his chest.

"Did she take much from you babe?" She asked in a soft but caring voice.

He looked at her, "It was enough so that she could analyze what effect that serum had on me." He then turned his head back to Shifter and then back to Stacey, "Look, I think that it would be best if we moved now Dr. Young's more than likely not aware of my escape just yet and that's the way I want to keep it for the time being."

They then started to move down the large corridor that connected the lab to the rest of the base, as they were walking Stacey looked back at him.

"Did Dr. Young hurt you?" She asked in a soft and caring voice.

Ben looked at her and smiled, "No, not at all. Why do you ask?" He said as they passed through an open door and turned left down another corridor.

Stacey gave him a puzzled look, "It's just I noticed those marks on the left of your face babe." Ben put his right hand across his cheek and felt the marks.

"Dr. Young scratched me, Stacey. But it didn't hurt," he said smiling.

As he did so Shifter turned his head, "Which part of the base is this security console located then boss?"

Ben smiled at him, "We just need to keep going on past this corridor Shamus it-"

As he said this they came up to a large doorway, inside was a large monitor and a console. The three of them looked at each other in amazement as they stepped inside, "now we all need to be very careful," He then said to both of them as they all stepped inside and started to look around,

"What are we looking for Ben?" Stacey asked as she turned towards him.

He then turned his head to her and Stacey could tell that he was afraid, "What Greena told me about this place and how to shut it down is that we need to find a large red button."

Shifter smiled as he turned towards back towards him, "You mean like that one over there boss?"

Ben then looked at it, sticking up in front of a monitor and out of a console was a large red button underneath it there was a large sign in red letters reading "don't not touch," all three mutants looked at one another and smiled,

"Looks like Greena was right after all boss." Shifter said as he smiled.

Ben turned to him and gave him a faint smile back.

"So who would like to do the honors?" Stacey asked as she put both of her hands across Ben's waist.

Ben turned his head slowly behind him and looked at her, "I think that you should be the one to push that button Stacey." He said as he gently held her one of her arms.

Stacey then let go of his waist and the made her way slowly to the console, as she did she could feel her whole body shaking, both Ben and Shifter looked at her as she took a few careful steps towards the console. As she held out her hand she felt it trembling as she reached out to push the button ignoring it she slammed her hand against the button, for a moment there was nothing then as if be magic the monitors started flickering off. Ben came forward and put one of his hands on Stacey's shoulders.

"Well done Stacey," he said in an encouraging voice, "Now let's contact Frostbite and the rest of Haven."

Stacey turned and smiled at him as she took his hand, all three of them then left the room laughing and smiling knowing that in just a few hours the base would be nothing but rubble.

CHAPTER THIRTY SIX

Captured

It was mid-morning as Frostbite was sitting by the table in the meeting room both of his arms were folded and there was a worried look on his face, sat beside him was Mist on one side and Powerhouse on the other. All three of them were growing impatient.

"Hey Frostbite." Mist said as she was reaching over towards a large jug of water that had been placed on the table, "Do you think that Green Girl and Shifter have managed to rescue Ben yet?"

Frostbite gave her a worried look, "I don't know Mist." he said as he got up from his chair and walked over towards a window.

e quickly turned his head towards her and Powerhouse, as he did this the mobile phone that he kept in his jacket pocket started ringing loudly,

"Frostbite here." he said in a heavy Russian accent as he picked it up and answered it. As Frostbite said this a familiar voice spoke to him.

"Hello old friend," it said in an English accent, "I am sorry that I kept you waiting."

Both Mist's and Powerhouse's eyes lit up as they both saw a smile spread across Frostbites face.

"Ben," Frostbite said in surprise, "I take it that you have escaped then?"

Ben then let out a soft laugh, "I did thanks to both Stacey and Shamus,"

Frostbite let out a laugh, "So I take it that you have managed to shut down the security system as well?"

Ben then let out another laugh, "You worry too much Sergei," he said as he smiled down the phone, "That's all been taken care of and I have some more news for you." Ben then paused for a moment as he turned towards Stacey who gave him a smile. "I have found and copied a list of chemicals that we used in that serum that created us."

Hearing this Frostbite grasped in shock, "What?! Seriously Ben?"

He smiled again, "Seriously Frostbite," he said as both himself, Stacey and Shifter ran into a room containing weapons and armor.

"Look, Sergei." he said as all three of them sat down on a bench to rest, "We can talk about this later, right now assemble all members of Haven and meet us inside this armory if you can."

As Frostbite was about to say something back the phone went dead, he then turned and faced Mist who was now walking slowly up to him smiling.

"So Ben's out of danger then?" She said her voice was calm and gentle.

Frostbite looked at her and gave her a nod, he then turned his head around to face Powerhouse who was now stood up.

"Powerhouse, Mist." he said as they both came towards him, "Gather the other members of Haven we are going hunting ourselves."

They both smiled and turned towards the door and downstairs leaving Frostbite on his own. Inside the armory Ben, Stacey and Shifter were breathing heavily, Shifter turned towards Ben and smiled. "That was easy enough wasn't it boss?"

He then turned his head towards the small man and gave him a smile.

"If you ask me that was too easy." Stacey said as she looked at them both her face looked afraid with fear, "Ben aren't you worried that this might have been a trap set up by Dr. Young?"

Ben looked at her and smiled, "You worry too much, Stacey," he said as got up and made his way toward a heavy locker, "Thanks to you we have shut down this bases security system thus effecting their communications, leaving them vulnerable and helpless so how could we be walking into a tr-?"

As he was about to finish something cut him off mid-sentence, he then turned his head towards Stacey and his face was frozen with fear.

"Oh my God," he said in a low voice, "I can sense human soldiers they are coming this way."

Stacey gave him a hard look, "See? I told you that it was too easy now what are we going to do?"

Shifter looked at them both, "We can always try to fight our way out of here."

Ben turned and looked at him giving him a hard look, "What fight the whole damn army Shamus? You must be out of your mind!"

As he was saying this all three of them frozen as they heard footsteps coming from outside the armory, Ben closed his eyes and scanned the minds of the soldiers that were waiting outside the door, Stacey slowly grabbed his arm and cuddled up to him, as she was doing this his eyes flicked open. Ben's breathing quicken as Shifter came forward.

"Well, how many of them are there boss?" He asked in a low frighten voice.

Ben turned towards him and his face was pale with fear, "Twenty-five solders if not more Shamus." He said trying not to alarm them both, "All of them are armed with AK47's,"

Stacey looked at him. "So we ended up rescuing you only to be captured ourselves?" She said in an angry voice.

Ben turned to her and gave her a faint smile, "Don't worry Stacey, I have an idea," as he was saying this they all heard the sound of heavy footsteps coming from outside the armor.

"Well, well, well" said a voice that he was familiar with, "So you did manage to escape." It said as the footsteps grew louder, as they grew louder a figure slowly enter the armory.

"Watts," Ben shouted in surprise, as he slowly came into the armory a squad of solder slowly came in from behind.

John looked at the three mutants standing before him and smiled, he then slowly came up to Stacey and put his hand around her neck. "So this is the green-skinned bitch who Dr. Young had all that trouble with oh so long ago."

"Let her go, Watts." Ben said angrily as he clenched his fists.

"Or else what?" Watts said as he let go of her neck, "As you can see Fox, you and your little group are surrounded, make one wrong move and all three of you will be as good as dead."

Shifter who was standing next to him walked slowly up to Watts.

"You piece of human filth," he said in an angry voice as he raised his hand, "You are nothing but a waste a disease that needs to be-."

As he said this Watts pulled out a small handgun out from a holster at his side and held it up to Shifter's chest.

"You scum talk too much," he said as he pulled the trigger.

There was a loud bang as Shifter's body fell to the ground, seeing this both Ben and Stacey ran over to him, Stacey then put her hand over his chest and looked at Ben.

"Babe, is he dead?" She asked him as she started sobbing over his body.

Ben then looked at her and nodded, then he turned at looked at Watts, "Why did you do that?! He wasn't even a threat to you and yet you shot him!"

Watts looked at him and gave him an evil smile, "You freaks should know your place in this world, Fox. you were created to be used in warfare." As he was saying this he pointed his gun at Ben, "Do you want to die next Fox or should I kill your green girlfriend?"

Ben looked at him and gave him an angry look, he then turned to face Stacey who was still sobbing over Shifter's body. "No Watts, no one else has to die here we both surrender."

Watts smiled at this as he turned towards a soldier who came behind him, "Slap them in cuffs and take them to Dr. Young. She will be delighted to see both of these freaks."

The solder did as he was told and put both them both in handcuffs, they then were both moved out of the armory and into the main corridor, as they were both moving towards a lift Ben's eyes began to glow Stacey watched as it looked to her like he was having another vision.

CHAPTER THIRTY SEVEN

Ben's failures

Stacey looked at Ben nervously as they stood in the lift surrounded by five soldiers, it had only been a few minutes since both of them had witness Shifter been killed in cold blood by Lieutenant Watts, since then both of them had been led away by him and a small squad of soldiers and forced into a lift which was now slowly taking them to the bases top floor where Dr. Young was waiting for them both. As the lift slowly crawled up to the third floor both Stacey and Ben looked at each other.

"Ben," Stacey whispered, "Ben, are you alright?" She asked her voice was soft and sad.

"Shut up you green-skinned freak," shouted Lieutenant Watts in a loud voice.

Stacey had almost forgotten that Shifter's killer was in the lift with them. Watts was standing at the front near the lift's doors. As he said this he slowly turned towards Stacey and walked over to her slowly holding up his handgun, whilst doing this he tried to avoid Ben's gaze.

"See this gun? asay anything else to your boyfriend beside you." He said as he held the gun up to her chest, "I'll use it to kill both you and your boyfriend if you try to escape or if you say another word so don't piss me off you green-skinned bitch!"

Stacey clenched both of her hands as he said this thinking back to when he shot Shifter in cold blood, as she was thinking about him her mind started to wander and she started to think that maybe Ben or her could or would be next to die. As she was thinking about the future the lift stopped as it reached the third floor, as the doors slowly opened Lieutenant Watts was the first to step out, as he stepped he quickly turned towards the five soldiers that had been behind them both.

"Okay men, listen up!" Watts said as he held the doors of the lift with one of his hands, "Dr. Young wants these two freaks unharmed and alive but if they both try anything funny then you are all authorized to use extreme methods, do I make myself clear?"

"Sir, yes sir!" they all shouted

"Good. Now lets get these freaks to Dr. Young," he said smiling,

Stacey felt one solder putting his hands on her back, he then gave her a push that nearly sent her flying out of the lift, as she went flying she turned towards Ben and noticed a solder hitting him with the butt of his gun around his face. He didn't do anything as blood poured down his face he only looked up at the young man,

"Stop that solder," came Watts' voice, "Dr. Young wants him as he is not damaged."

The soldier looked at Watts and stopped what he was doing. Standing there the solder looked at Watts and gave a salute.

"You two," Watts growled at two soldiers who were just standing in the lift, "Take Fox along with that green-skinned freak into Dr. Young's private office, try and patch him up."

The two young men gave a salute and walked over to Ben who was now sat on the ground his face covered in blood,

"Alright," one of them said, "on your feet."

They then grabbed him by both of his arms and carried him down a corridor. Stacey again felt someone's hands around her back, she quickly turned her head around to face her attacker, as she did this she came face to face with a young black soldier.

"Move it you bitch!" He said in an aggressive voice.

Ytacey couldn't do anything as both of her hands were still in handcuffs she only gave the young man a hard and cold look as he pushed her out towards the corridor. They had only been walking down the corridor for a few minutes when without warning they both turned left and entered a door, as Stacey was pushed thought she could see that the room she had now entered was different from the rest of the base. At the far side there was an oak desk on the desk there was a large laptop computer and a large leather office chair, Stacey also noticed that the walls in the room were painted red, she then knew that this wasn't a military installation it was Dr. Young's private office. Stacey then was pushed again and this time landed onto the floor, as this happened the young soldier that has pushed her rushed back out and locked the door, Stacey turned her head to the right and found Ben, he was sitting by the desk on a small wooden chair, Stacey got back up to her feet and walked slowly up to him.

"Ben," she asked in a soft voice, "Are you alright, babe?" He then turned towards her and gave her a sad look.

"I've failed Stacey," she looked at him and put on of her hands on his shoulders.

"What do you mean, babe?" She asked him and her voice was soft,

Ben lowered his head and for the first time in his life since he became a mutant felt guilty, "I let Shamus die, I also let you get captured and now God knows what Young is going to do with us both." Stacey sat down beside him and touched his face with her hand, as she was doing this Ben still couldn't believe how smooth her green skin was.

"Ben," she said in a gentle voice, "That wasn't your fault what happened to Shifter, it was Watts he is-"

Before she could say anything they both stood up from where they were sitting as they heard the door been unlocked, Ben turned to her and from the look on his face she could tell that he was worried, Ben turned his head towards her and then to the door watching as the handler turned. He then turned his head back round to her.

"Whatever comes out of that door, be ready," he said in a worried voice, Stacey turned her head towards him.

"Who do you think it is Ben?" She asked in a low and worried voice, he looked at her. "I sense Dr. Young and a few soldiers with her and there is someone else but I can't tell who they are."

They then both turned back to the door which was now half open. Now both of them grew afraid.

CHAPTER THIRTY EIGHT

The Revenge of the Mega humans

Stacey and Ben were both in shock as they both saw Dr. Young and a few solders appearing from behind the door, as she made her way into the room she glared at him and showed Stacey an evil smile, she then made her way towards the chair at her desk and sat down the solders that had followed her in lined up against the wall as she did this.

"Hello Stacey," she said as she sat down on the leather chair, "How nice to see you again."

Stacey didn't say anything at first to her she just gave her a cold look and started grinding her teeth.

"You are more than likely going to ask me what it is that I want to do with you?" Dr. Young asked her in a soft but unfriendly voice.

Stacey gave her another hard look but this time she slammed her hand down on the desk and clinched one of her hands into a fist.

"Why are you so interested in ruining my life?" She asked in an aggressive voice. "Van't you see that Ben, myself and the other mutants that you created only want to live in peace?"

As she was saying this the solders that were lined up against the wall pointed their guns at her and were preparing to open fire on her, Dr. Young then raised one of her hands and order them to stand down.

"My dear Stacey," she said in a mocking tone, "You, your boyfriend here, and the rest of the other mutants are worth far too much to just let you go like that, like I said before when we both met that time the military is in need of super solders to help us win wars over seas."

As Stacey heard this her face dropped. "It tall all we are to you then? Bothing but cannon fodder?"

A smile appeared on Dr. Young's face, "As your boyfriend has more than likely told you that some mutants are hardier than others, take you, for example, you have a super healing factor that lets your body heal wounds that could otherwise be fatal to a normal human." She then sat up from her chair and went over to the window that looked out to the sea, she then quickly turned back to Stacey, "Imagine Stacey, the lives that could be saved in war thanks to people like yourself."

Ben then looked up at Dr. Young, "You're nothing but a monster Dr. Falsely! Advertising a product to young people only for them to become experiments to be used by both the British and American Governments for warfare."

Dr. Young came slowly up to him and slapped him around his face. "Too many innocent people die in warfare, too many precious troops are getting killed on the battlefield this is my answer to our problem!"

Stacey didn't say anything she just turned her head and looked at Ben. Ever since Shifter had been killed he had gone into a state of depression blaming himself for his death and also for his and Stacey's capture, the once strong young mutant that Stacey had known was gone replaced by a shell, Stacey then turned her head back round to Dr. Young who was now smiling at them both. She stood up and looked at her, her eyes were full of rage,/

"What do you intend to do with us both now then Doctor?" She asked.

Dr. Young then showed her a smile, "Isn't it obvious my dear? I intend to hand you over to the British military."

"And what about Ben, where is he going?" She asked in an angry tone.

Dr. Young went back over to her desk and sat down, "Ben is staying here at this base." As she was saying this he then started laughing out loud, "What's so funny, freak?"

One of the soldiers said as he held his rifle up to his head, Ben looked at the man and gave him a smile, then he turned towards Dr. Young.

"No one is going anywhere, Young." He said in an angry tone.

Dr. Young looked at him, "And why is that, Ben?" She asked him in a mocking tone.

He then smiled at her showing her a set of stained yellow teeth, "because the cavalry is on their way that why."

Without warning the room was filled with a blue colored smoke, emerging from the smoke came Frostbite, Mist, Powerhouse, Violet, and flamethrower. Dr. Young's face dropped as she saw them she then turned to face him.

"You little bastard," she said and her face was red with rage, "You planned this all along didn't you?"

Ben smiled at her, "Not just me, Doctor. I had a little help from a friend of mine,"

Dr. Young then looked at the soldiers, "What are you waiting for?! All of you open fire!" She screamed as she ran out of the room.

Frostbite looked at the solders as he stretched out both of his hands and let out an icy blast, freezing them all before they had a chance to open fire. He then walked slowly up to Ben and Stacey, Ben looked at him and smiled, "You're late as usual, what kept you?"

Frostbite smiled as he touched the handcuffs around his wrist freezing them, Ben broke them off his hands letting them shatter to the floor. Frostbite then did the same to Stacey's, as soon as he did this he turned to Ben.

"Where's Shifter Ben?" He asked in a worried voice, Ben looked at him and his head was lowered, "I am afraid Shifter won't be joining us, as he was killed."

"How?! Who killed him?!" Mist asked as she held up one of her handguns.

He then looked at her and then turned his gaze towards the rest of his followers, "Watts shot him, there was nothing that me or Stacey could do."

Frostbite looked at his friend and then looked towards the door, "Ben, I know that you have done your best for us all, but I think that's it's now time for revenge."

Ben looked at him friend and gave a faint smile, "I agree with you on this one Frostbite, but let's not forget that we have two targets now Dr Young and Lt Watts."

Violet came up to him and put a hand on his shoulder.

"What are your orders Ben?" she asked her voice was soft and gentle.

Ben turned towards the purple skinned woman and smiled, "Normally, I wouldn't say this, but we need to kill both Young and Watts before they can do anymore harm or damage." he then looked over at Stacey who was now standing near him. He then slowly walked over to her and placed a hand over one of her shoulders.

"Stacey," he said softly, "Are you with me on this one?"

Stacey looked at him and then looked over at the frozen bodies of the soldiers in the corner of the room.

"Yes Ben," Ahe said as she turned to face him, "I'm with you."

CHAPTER THIRTY NINE

The meeting with Watts

Dr. Young could feel herself getting angry as she was getting out of the lift since the other mutants had arrived the base has descended into chaos.

"It's all that bitch Greena's fault." she said to herself as she made her way towards the bases command center.

aA she passed through the door she noticed Lt Watts and a few other soldiers standing around at a monitor observing what was happening, hearing her entering the room John turned towards her with a sour look on his face.

"What happened down there Doctor? Why is this base now under attack from those mutants?" He asked her in an angry tone/

She looked at him and then lowered her head.

"We have been betrayed." she said in a low soft voice.

"Whose the traitor?!" Watts shouted angrily.

Dr. Young looked away from him in fear as she had never seen him lose his temper.

"I think that it's agent Greena who has done this." She said in a fearful voice.

"What makes you say that Sarah?" Watts asked again as he turned his back on her and looked at the monitor.

Dr. Young chewed her lower lip, "I heard Fox saying that him and his followers had help."

Watts quickly turned his head back towards her and walked slowly up to her.

"What makes you say this about one of our most loyal agents?" He asked as he reached out and made a grab for her neck, as he was about to do this his radio that he kept in his side pocket began to buzz, he then picked it up and answered it ignoring her as he walked over to the monitor, "Watts here." he said in a calm voice.

"Lieutenant," came the voice of a young soldier, "Thank God! We're under attack, hostiles have taken the armory on the third floor."

Watts lowered the radio and looked over at Dr. Young who now had a worried look on her face, he then lifted it back up to his mouth. "Stay cool son, I'll send reinforcements your way."

"Negative sir, there is no-" as the solder was about to finish his sentence there a scream followed by a deathly silence."

Watts looked at Dr. Young and then shouted into the radio, "Soilder, are you there?! Respond!"

At first there was no answer to a familiar voice answered, "Hello there Lieutenant, How are you doing?"

Watts turned his head towards Dr. Young and from the look on his face he was in shock.

"Fox!" he snapped, Ben then started laughing as he heard his name being mentioned, "What's so damn funny freak?!" Watts shouted in panic.

Ben for a moment stopped as he turned his gaze to Stacey who was now standing next to him.

"You are almost out of time John," he said in a mocking tone.

"What do you mean by that freak and how many of my men have you killed?"

He the looked over at Stacey as he said this and then turned his head towards Greena behind her was a large number of soldiers in handcuffs, he then raised the radio back up to his mouth as he let out a smile. "John do you think that I am a cold-blooded killer?"

Watts lets out a laugh as he heard this, "Please, I know that you and the rest of your followers are nothing but murders and terrorists."

Hearing this Stacey snatched the radio out of Ben's hand, "The only murderer here is you! You're going to pay for what you did to Shifter you bastard."

Watts looked over to the window and let out another laugh, "Please don't make me laugh, you both think that you can win against me and my forces?"

Before they both could say anything else Watts turned the radio off and made his way towards Dr. Young who gave him a worried look.

"What?! Why are you giving me that look?" He asked her.

"John," she said in a soft voice, "I don't think that you or I should underestimate either Fox or his followers."

Watts laughed again, "What?! Do you think that I am afraud of him?" Before she could answer out of the vents came a thick blue colored vapor that settles in the middle of the room, as the vapor settle it took on the form of three figures one male and two females Ben, Stacey, and Mist. Dr. Young gasped and Lt watts grew angry as he saw them.

CHAPTER FORTY

End Game

Lt Watts face was red with rage as he saw standing a few yards away from him were Ben, Stacey, and Mist, he eyed them up as he though to himself that he must have been dreaming? As he did this Dr. Young slipped passed him and ran towards an escape hatch in the corner of the room, Ben stepped forward towards him, as he did this the three solders that had stood by the Lieutenant raised they weapons towards him, he then quickly turned and raised on of his hands towards the three men. As he did this one of the men went crashing into the monitor that Watts had been looking at early, seeing one of their own going down the other two opened fire, as the bullets came speeding towards him Ben raised one of his hands, as he did this they stopped mid air and fell harmlessly to the fall. As this was happening Watts decided to make his move, he came up behind him and got him in a choke hold.

"Not so hot now are you, Fox?" He said in a mocking tone

As this was happening both Stacey and Mist moved forward to try and help him but both of them were stopped by the two solders, Watts turned toward them and started laughing.

"That's right, freaks." he said in yet another mocking tone, "Back away now or else he dies."

Stacey looked at Mist giving her an angry look on her face, Mist gave her back a worried look.

"Green Girl," she said in a soft voice, "We better do as he says."

Ben then looked at them both, "Don't surrender yourselves on my account."

Stacey looked at him and gave him a sad look, "Why not Ben? If you die then we might as well all of us be dead." As she said this both her and Mist back away from both him and Watts.

As they both did this Watts nodded to both of the solders who had been standing next to him to take them away, both of them then came towards them both and in their hands were a par of handcuffs, as they were about to place them around their wrists they came what felt like an icy blast followed by someone shouting "Get out of the way!"

Hearing this Stacey and Mist got on their hands and knees and rolled out of the way. As they both did this they both noticed both solders been hit, as the blast hit them it frozen them both solid, Stacey knew who it was who was responsible for this and she was right. As both her and Mist got up from the ground they both noticed Frostbite walking towards them, with him was Greena and Powerhouse, all three of them looked tired and wore out from fighting, Watts' eyes glared as he saw all three of them coming into the room, his grip tighten around Ben's neck, Stacey made her way over to where Frostbite stood as he watched Watts and Ben. Frostbite looked at the two young women his eyes were cold and full of hate.

"Boy, I am glad to see you again Frostbite." Mist said as she came forward.

Stacey looked at him and gave him a worried look, "Where are Violet and Flamethrower?"

Greena came forward she was wearing a ripped army uniform and her red hair was matted with blood. "Both of them won't be joining us Green Girl, they were killed."

"They aren't going to be the only freaks dying today!" came a voice behind them.

Stacey turned and saw Watts still holding Ben in a choke hold, this time however in one of his hands was a small handgun pointed at his head. Watts looked at the mutants that were present in the room eyeing them up, "Surrender now or I'll blow Fox's brains out."

Frostbite looked at him and smiled, "You think that you can bully us Watts? Think again!"

Watts looked at Frostbite and laughed, "Do you freaks think that the USA army will go down without a fight? Just because you have taken over this base it will spur the rest of the military against you as you have committed an act of terrorism."

Stacey looked at him and gave him an angry look, "You're the one who has committed murder not us."

Watts looked at her in disgust, "Shut it you green skinned bitch." As he said he pointed the gun away from Ben head and aimed it at Stacey.

Seeing this Ben grew angry and with his free hand elbowed Watts in the chest winding him, as this happened Watts dropped the gun and let go of him. He then staggered around the room in pain, as this was happening he looked up at Ben who now was on his feet and looked straight into his eyes, Ben smiled as he raised one of his hands and began to peer inside Watts mind. With this happening Stacey rushed back to both Mist and Greena and watched as Watts slowly began to lost control of his mind and his will, ten minutes later Watts fell onto the floor as this happening Ben walked slowly up to his body and kneeled down.

"Your mind is mine now, Watts!" he said in an angry tone.

As he stood up he turned his head over to where Stacey and his followers were standing. He then ran over to her and they both threw their arms around one another, as she was resting her hand on his back she closed her eyes.

"Are you OK babe?" He asked her in a soft voice.

"Ben," she said in a gentle voice, "You knew what he was about to do didn't you?"

Ben then let go of her and looked at her, "Of course I did Stacey, that why I wanted to use myself as bait."

As he was saying this Frostbite put his hand on his shoulder, "Ben may I have a word please?"

Ben then looked at his friend and smiled faintly, "Of course Frostbite, what is it?"

Frostbite looked at him and Ben could tell that he was worried, "During our attack on this base I noticed that there was no sign of Dr. Young."

Greena came forward, "She must have escaped somehow."

Ben looked at them both and then looked over at Stacey, "At the moment we have bigger fish to fry than Dr. Young. Like for example, cleaning up this base." He then walked slowly up to Stacey and put his arm around her waist, "I'll get in touch with Peter later see if he can put a warrant out for her arrest."

They then left the room and went downstairs towards the exit, as they were leaving a male figure slowly emerged from the shadows, he began to watch them as Mist teleported them away with great interest, once they had left the figure pulled out a phone from out of a coat pocket.

"This is Watcher," he said in a Polish accent.

A male's voice spoke over the phone, "Great to hear from you Watcher. Were you successful in your mission?"

Watcher smiled as he heard this, "I was boss and you were right Armstrong is a bigger threat than we thought."

The voice over the phone went silent for a moment, then took out a deep breath, "Then you know what to do next, Watcher. Spy on both him and that group of his. Don't take your eye off that little girlfriend of his."

Watcher smiled at this, "Understood boss and thank you for trusting me."

The man then let out a laugh, "With the army now out of the picture and Dr Young on the run the Outcasts will have free roaming of Florida and soon the whole world."

Watcher then smiled and put the phone back into his coat pocket, he then walked slowly out of the base and onto the beach.

Printed in the United States
By Bookmasters